GRASSHOPPER SUMMER

ANN TURNER

GRASSHOPPER SUMMER

Troll Associates

A TROLL BOOK, published by Troll Associates

Published by arrangement with Macmillan Publishing Company, Inc.
For information address Macmillan Publishing Company, Inc.,
866 Third Avenue, New York, New York 10022.

First Troll Printing, 1991

Printed in the United States of America.

10 9 8 7

ISBN 0-8167-2262-5

For

my father,

with love

GRASSHOPPER SUMMER

CHAPTER ONE

I crouched beside the tarpaper shack. It smelled sour and old and damp. The winter wind blew in the dried cornstalks. It was the voices that brought me down here.

"C-a-t, cat, Harold, see that?"

"Yes, Mr. William, I do see that."

"And then this one." I heard chalk squeak on a slate. "M-a-t, mat. Same thing, Harold, except it begins with a *m*."

"Oh, yes, I do see that. And this is 'rat,' 'r-a-t,' rat!" Harold's voice got higher when he was excited.

I inched closer to the window and looked in. Billy crouched on the dirt floor by Harold, slate in hand. Harold held on to the slate like a drowning man on to a log. He repeated, "Rat, r-a-t, mat, m-a-t, cat, c-a-t! Well, Mr. William, you could teach a mouse to read."

Billy flicked his blond hair back from his eyes. He was smiling. "Oh, Harold, I could not. You made it easy."

Harold sighed. "Just think of it, Mr. William. Once a slave, now I can read. There's no telling what I can do with it. Why, you know I've still got a wife down Georgia way. . . ." His voice trailed off.

Billy patted his knee. "I know, Harold, I know. Maybe you'll be able to send for her one day."

"Maybe, maybe." Harold rubbed his face. "But I do know this, if things'll ever get better, we've got to know how to read."

"That's right, Harold." Billy wiped the slate clean with his sleeve.

It was quiet for a moment. I sucked in a breath. If Grandpa knew what Billy was doing—that sneak! Coming down here to Harold's shack and teaching a slave to read! Well, an ex-slave, anyway, and what did he need to read for?

Suddenly, I ran up the path and whistled. I didn't want him to see me, 'cause that was just the lowest of the low to spy on someone, even your younger brother.

A minute later, he came out of the shack, rubbing his eyes in the brightness. "Yes, Sam?"

He was being polite, the way he always was when he was mad at me. "What you doing down there at Harold's shack?" I said. "You know Grandpa said to stay away from there. He said you're a big boy now, ten years old"—I went up and shook his arm—"too big to be friends with a slave."

"Ex-slave, Sam," Billy said automatically. He came with me up the path to the house. It was one of the things I hated about Billy. He didn't fight. If you grabbed his arm, he'd come. If you yelled at him, he'd never shout back.

Ta-da, ta-da! Grandpa was on the porch blowing his bugle.

"Stupid old bugle," Billy muttered, drawing his arm away.

I stopped. "Stupid? Who're you calling stupid? What's stupid is trying to teach a slave to read, that's what! You might as well just pour water into a river for all the good it'll do him."

Billy looked at me. Those eyes made me jittery, blue and bright as marbles.

"Well, it *is* stupid," I repeated.

"Says you! I like Harold. I like teaching him to read. If you tell Grandpa about us, I'll tell him about that time you, Jeb, and Luke got into Pa's corn liquor in the barn and got so sick."

"You wouldn't!"

"I would, too," he nodded. "I most certainly

would, Samuel T. White. 'Sides, Harold knows something *you* don't know." Billy waltzed ahead of me, under the big linden tree. He patted Jake's yellow head for a second, pulling softly on his ears. Jake nudged him and whined.

"What does *he* know?"

Billy turned and put his hands in his pockets. He drew out something furry. "See this, Sam? It's a rabbit's foot."

"So?"

"Harold gave it to me—to *me*, Samuel T. White, for the journey we'll be going on." Billy turned and walked on.

"What journey?" I ran to catch up and grabbed his shoulder.

Billy faced me. "Well, Harold's not exactly *sure*. . . ."

"I bet he's not sure!" I snapped.

"Not exactly sure just where we're going, but he says we'll be leaving soon. He said, 'Your pa's so restless he's wearing tracks in that road going back and forth to town. He'll be traveling on, and you'll all go with him.' "

I took a deep breath. We couldn't be going anywhere, no matter what Harold said. Just 'cause Pa was going into town a lot these days didn't mean anything. How could he want to leave Kentucky?

"Where, I'd like to know?" I planted my feet wide and put my hands on my hips. If I were a sergeant and Billy a soldier, I could make him answer.

Billy walked on, humming under his breath. He *knew* how that got to me, those little hums.

"Where?" I caught up and grabbed him.

He took my hand and pulled it off his shoulder. "It doesn't matter where, Sam, don't you know that by now? Harold says you got 'eyes like a hawk and ears like rocks,' that's what he says, and he's right."

"What does that man know? Living in a shack at the bottom of our field?"

"He knows things, Sam." Billy walked slower, and Jake kept close to his knee. "He sees things."

I shivered. Harold couldn't be right. I'd never leave this house with Grandpa and Grandma inside. The bugle sounded again. *Ta-da, ta-da!* As always.

"Always!" I said out loud.

"What's that, Sam?"

"Grandpa will always blow his bugle for mealtimes. Grandma will always bake peach pies and cool them on the sill. Ma will always go visiting friends in her black buggy. Pa will always plant the fields."

Billy was silent for a moment, scratching Jake's ear. He mounted the steps and said over his shoulder, "Harold says there's no such thing as always."

CHAPTER TWO

THE NEXT MORNING WAS WILD AND WINDY. Doves called in the linden tree as Billy and I set off for school.

"Remember to do what the teacher says," Grandma called after me.

"Yes, ma'am, I always do." I grinned at her. She was neat and tidy in her white apron. Her hair was pulled back so tight it looked like it hurt.

"You do not," Billy said, jumping down the steps ahead of me.

I reached out to grab his blue coat, but I saw Pa in the yard, swinging his leg up over Justin. The gelding pranced and shied.

"Where're you going, Pa?" I called.

"Into town, Sam." He pulled in the reins and pushed his hat down on his head. His brown hair stuck out from under the brim, and his red beard bristled. He looked the way I feel when school is let out for the summer.

"And what're you going to do there, Pa?" Billy and I started down the road toward school, with Pa keeping Justin to a slow walk beside us.

"I'm going to find the future, boys, find the future!" Pa grinned at us, dug his heels into Justin's side, and leaped off, mud spurting onto our jackets.

"Will you look at that! We can't go to school all muddy, Billy!"

"We can't?" He smiled at me. I didn't understand why his smile made me feel mean.

"Wipe it off with your hankie." Billy wiped his sleeves and set off down the road. I dabbed at the mud. But I had more to worry about than that. Pa. Going to town every day. Talking about the future and waving pieces of paper covered with writing in Ma's face. Maybe Billy and Harold were right. Just yesterday Ma smiled and shook her head, and I heard him say, "I've got it all figured out, Ellen." Whatever "all" was. I pulled my collar up and jammed my hands into my pockets. I did wish I were a soldier. Soldiers have rules, and they know what's coming.

When we got to school, Billy slid into his seat next to Milly Daily. The only boy in the *entire* school to sit next to a girl. It was just like being friends with Harold—not right. I took my seat next to Jeb and sighed.

"What's wrong?" he asked.

I did like that Jeb. His flat red hair, like mine, his nice, comfy face.

"Nothing," I opened my book and pretended to read. "Nothing at all, Jeb."

"Well, that's good. I could've sworn that somebody just died, Sam."

I tried to smile. If Billy and Harold were right about Pa, then I'd have to leave Jeb and Luke. And leave the best catfish river in the country.

Mrs. Thorne rapped her ruler on the desk and called the little ones up to say their letters. I didn't see them; all I saw was Pa looking wild and happy, galloping to town. The mud spurted up, Billy handed me his hankie, and Pa disappeared down the road. Over and over again. And no matter how many times I saw it inside, I couldn't change it, couldn't make Pa come back to us.

"Samuel T. White!"

"Samuel T. White!"

I shook my head at the pesky words and woke up a bit. "Yes'm?" I didn't like what I saw. Ten rows of dead hard chairs and desks all filled with boys and girls. Mrs. Thorne at the head of the schoolroom with a ruler in her hand. She rapped it on the desk.

"Samuel, read the beginning of page five, *if* you please."

How can it be that some grown-ups say "please" and it sounds like a swear?

"Yes'm," I said, and began to read. My tongue stumbled on the words. I knew them, all right; it was just reading in front of all those people. I began to sweat, and the words blurred on the page. I felt like I was pushing rocks out of my mouth. Someone snickered in back. I turned around fast. It was silly old Roger with a face like a crumbled pie. He laughed at anything, and I whipped my head back and tried to read again.

I got slower and slower until Mrs. Thorne said, "That will be all, Samuel. Work on your reading at home. You should be reading better, a boy of your age."

The sweat trickled down my shirt collar. Billy sat two seats away. He had his head straight ahead and didn't look like he was laughing at me. But you never could tell—with Billy. Why was it that he could read fast and I couldn't? I could do sums just fine. I didn't see how we could be brothers, we were so different.

I bent my head over my books and pretended to read, scraping my fingernail against the slate. It screeched. All the girls jumped and Mrs. Thorne grabbed the edge of her desk.

"Who did that?"

No one answered. She couldn't know it was me, but she did give me a long, hard look. I just sighed, like I was tired from reading so hard. After a time I looked around. Jeb nudged me, and Luke grinned. I tried to read but it was no use. I kept hearing Pa's words, "I'm going to find the future, boys!"

CHAPTER THREE

I WALKED HOME FAST. Jeb thumped my shoulder when he got to his road, and Luke waved goodbye. I could hear Billy laughing behind me. I whipped around fast and stared.

He handed Milly Daily her lunch pail and waved good-bye. "It's not my fault you got in trouble in school, Sam."

I glared at him and took a step. He spread his hands wide.

"It's not my fault. I wasn't laughing at you, Sam, honest!"

"You'd better not be!" I turned around and walked fast back home. I didn't feel like talking to Billy— Mr. Do-Good, Mr. Read-It-Fast William.

When we got home, he went in to talk with Grandma, the way he always did. When I was younger and something bad happened, I'd sit with Grandma in the kitchen. She'd give me a piece of pie, polish up her tiny glasses, and say, "What's wrong, Sam?" But a time comes when you have to stop telling your troubles. Soldiers don't tell their troubles to their grandmothers.

Instead, I went upstairs. I knew I wasn't supposed to. Pa *said* to stay away from his trunk and his things from the war, but I just had to open that lid.

Inside, it smelled musty. Underneath a gray blanket was Pa's army jacket. I took it out and put it on.

Stiff, gray sleeves with stains on them. Bright buttons marching up the front. I wondered if Pa polished those buttons, they were so bright. I fastened the top one and the stiff collar held me up. Made me feel taller, bigger than Mrs. Thorne and those silly people in school.

I saw Ma in the hallway below, drawing off her gloves. I waited until she took off her hat and went into the kitchen. Didn't want her to see me in Pa's jacket; didn't want any questions about my day in school.

Downstairs, I grabbed an old ax handle and ran outside. Clouds were blowing away like gray rags on a washing line.

—

12

I stalked out over the field, shooting at some doves and dropping out of sight behind a bush. It sure was lonely with the doves calling and the wind shushing in the cornstalks.

Grandpa strode toward me.

"Fighting, son?"

I stood, kind of shamefaced. "No, sir, just—practicing."

"Don't let your pa see you, son. He won't like you wearing that jacket."

"No, sir."

"Well, this is how you do it." He took the ax handle from me. "Flat against your shoulder, and at the ready when you see the enemy." I didn't need to ask who the enemy was—Yankees.

He dropped to his knee and I followed. "Snug that rifle butt into your shoulder and sight along the barrel. Then fire!"

Grandpa's eyes blazed. I moved aside to give him room.

"Then reload, up against the shoulder, and fire again. And don't you move until your commanding officer tells you to!"

"No, sir! Grandpa, did you shoot lots of Yankees in the war?"

He stood, straightening his jacket. He always was neatly dressed and buttoned up like a soldier. He wore his gray hair long to his shoulders, and his gray beard came to a point.

"I shot some—enough. I did what my government ordered me to do—that's what a good soldier does. And look, Sam!" He swept his arm across the farmland. I saw the brown fields like soft blankets stretching away. I saw the empty slave houses down by the river, though Pa said we never had that many slaves. I saw the low red barn with only two horses left in it. "They took twenty acres of my best bottom land after the war and burned the rest." He spat to one side. "But I'd do it all over again. We were right and the right side lost."

A hand on my shoulder made me jump.

"What are you doing with my jacket on?"

"Just—just practicing, Pa, with Grandpa. If I'm ever going to get my own rifle, I have to know what to do, don't I?" I got real quiet then. He didn't look wild and happy the way he had this morning, going off on Justin. Now his eyes squinted, his mouth was tight, and it was my fault for wearing that old jacket.

Pa gave me a look I didn't understand and glared at Grandpa. "Take the jacket off—this minute!"

"Walter," Grandpa protested, "he's only. . . ."

"Playing at war, Colonel, playing at war! I won't have it." He took the jacket from me and folded it carefully. "Those days are gone, dead and gone these nine years. This is a new world, and we've all got to get used to it."

"It's not a *better* world," Grandpa fired back.

I stepped between them. Grandpa's words pulled me one way, Pa's words the other, and it hurt.

Pa pushed me aside. "It *is* better, Colonel, for a man with vision, that is." His voice was sharp. Softer, he said, "Davy didn't have vision." He touched the stains on the jacket's sleeve.

I was too scared to ask about Davy. Pa never talked about the war.

"What did Davy get for being a good soldier?" Pa held up the jacket and shook it. "That's his blood on the sleeve. He died next to me in a ditch where I lay for three nights and three days."

Three days and three nights! I clenched my fists.

"I know, Walter." Grandpa touched his arm. "I know that was a long, terrible time."

Pa shook off his hand. "You don't know the half of it, Colonel! Never again, never again." He spat to one side and wiped his mouth. Then he kicked the earth so hard a clod flew up to one side. "I tell you, I hate this land now."

"Walter!"

"I do. It's full of blood, and it's old and tired, and times come it almost suffocates me!" Pa pulled at his collar, and his beard bristled. I was too scared to move, to speak. He stalked off toward the house, the jacket close to his chest.

Grandpa patted me on the shoulder. "Don't you mind, Sam, don't you mind."

I trembled under Grandpa's hand. I'd never heard Pa speak that way before.

"Don't you mind, Sam." Grandpa cleared his throat. "Sometimes men in battle don't forget and it gnaws at them. Remember, when something bad happens you just forget about it. Don't hold on to it like your father."

Maybe that time lying in the ditch was why Pa had those dark days. When his face would be all pale and solemn and we could do nothing right, not even Billy.

A crow flew overhead making that mournful noise. "Do you think, Grandpa . . ."

"What's that, son?" Grandpa started. He was staring across the river.

"About Pa . . . about going into town." I couldn't get the words out.

"Doesn't mean a thing, son!" Grandpa tried to smile at me.

"Then, do you think I could have a rifle this year, Grandpa? One of my own?" I rubbed my arms. Everything would be the same. I'd get my rifle and go hunting with Jeb and Luke. Ma would go visiting in the buggy, Grandma would make peach pies,

Grandpa would blow his bugle at mealtimes, and Billy would be a pest—as always.

When Grandpa didn't answer, I touched his arm. He did not look at me and pulled on his beard. "Maybe, Sam, maybe this year. We'll see what happens."

CHAPTER FOUR

ON FRIDAY NIGHT BILLY GOT DOWN ON HIS hands and knees and began to pull things out of his maple dresser and throw them on the floor.

"What're you doing?" I asked.

"Getting ready." Jake came into our room, his toenails clicking. He sat next to Billy, leaning his head forward for a scratch.

"Good boy, Jake," Billy patted him and then hugged him tight. "Oh, I will miss you, you old dog, you. I guess you won't be coming with us." Billy sniffed.

"Why can't he?" Then I almost kicked myself. I was talking like I believed him. "We're not going anywhere. You're just crazy to get your things in a mess for nothing."

"Sure, Sam." Billy bent down and pulled a canvas sack out from under the bed. "You just go on that way and see where it gets you. Harold says—"

"Harold says!" I jumped up and went to the dark window. I couldn't see anything; only the rain hissed against the panes. "Harold! What does *that* man know about Pa or anything else?"

"He knows, is all, Sam."

"Stuff!" I rubbed the wet glass. I looked for a break in the clouds with a star so I could wish, "Don't let us leave—ever."

Billy pulled out his plaid shirts, two pairs of winter pants and a summer pair, one flannel nightgown, a winter jacket, and two caps. On top he put his collection of arrowheads.

"And what're you going to do with *those*?" I picked up an arrowhead and tossed it.

"Give it here, Sam!" Billy made a snatch for it.

"You going to trade these with the Indians?" I danced around, and Jake leaped beside me.

"Give it back, Sam!" Billy grabbed my hand, and we tumbled down onto his pile of clothing. I kept my hand just out of reach, and suddenly, Billy jumped up and straightened his clothes.

"Okay, Sam, you just go on that way. See where it gets you. Pretend we're not going anywhere. Act like a fool. I don't care."

"Who's acting like a fool, I'd like to know?" I

stood, but Billy didn't back away, and he didn't say anything more. What's the use of fighting with someone who won't talk and won't move? I tossed the arrowhead back onto the pile.

"Time for bed, boys!" Ma called from the hallway. "Hurry up, now."

"Aw, Ma, I'm not done yet," Billy said. He was still stuffing things into that dratted sack of his.

Ma came to the doorway. Made me feel calm just to see her: her soft brown eyes, the brown dress that fell in folds to her tiny, polished boots. She smiled at me.

"Sam, you look all cross and jittery. Is anything wrong?"

"Yes." I pointed to Billy. "He's packing, that's what's wrong."

"Why are you packing, William?"

"Because Harold says we're going on a long journey, Ma. He said, 'Your poor mother'll cross many a river before *she* comes to rest.' " He knelt back on his heels.

Ma fidgeted with her lace collar. "Well, now, nothing's been decided, boys, nothing at all, at least . . ."

"That's good! I told you we weren't going anywhere, Billy. See, Ma said, nothing's been decided."

Billy kept packing.

"It's just—your father *is* getting restless. I don't know." She smoothed back her hair and looked so weary all of a sudden. I went over and hugged her. I could smell the lavender she always wore. Everything would be all right.

She kissed me lightly on the head and said, "Get into bed and blow out the candle."

We did as she told us to, and Ma kissed Billy first, then me. "'Night, boys." Softly, she closed the door. The dog pawed Billy's blanket, sighed, and lay down.

"I get Jake tomorrow night, hear?" I wished I had him right that minute, warm and cozy on my legs.

"Okay, Sam, but it won't make any difference. We're still leaving. And you'll still hate to go."

"And you won't?"

"No, Sam, I like adventure. I like changes—not like you." Jake sighed and whuffed.

"Ma *said* nothing's been decided."

"Who decides things around here?"

Grandpa. Pa. Certainly not Ma. The rain hissed on the window and Jack scratched a flea.

I couldn't talk anymore. I could feel change coming like a cold wind. I shivered in bed, pulled the blanket up to my chin, and stared at the dark.

———

"WELL? Are we going West or aren't we? Is anyone going to tell me?" I looked around the table

———

21

the next night, at the blue plates set so neat, at all of us washed and brushed for dinner.

Pa's knife clattered on the plate. Grandpa choked and shook his head. Ma kept pushing peas around on her plate.

"Yes, Sam, we're going West." Pa wiped his mouth and smiled.

Billy grinned and mouthed, "See?"

"Where, Pa? Where are we going?"

"Dakota Territory, Sam."

"But, Pa, that's North! We'll be Southerners up North!" The peas felt like pebbles in my mouth.

"That doesn't matter anymore, Sam. It's a new time, a new place—opportunity"—he waved his fork—"fresh lands. Not all worn and used up like—"

"We're not all worn and used up!" Grandma jammed her eyeglasses against her face.

"No, no, of course not, I didn't mean that, Mother," Pa said.

"He means we can make a fresh start there," Ma said softly.

"What about a fresh start here?" Grandpa pulled on his beard. "We're recovering from the war now. We need young men with good ideas."

"Thank you, Colonel, but I've made up my mind. We've been over this all before. It's too good a chance, and now the farm's smaller, and prices are lower, it's hard to make a living here." Pa clasped his hands. "But out there, we have a chance to make our own way."

"My cousin Millie says"—Grandma set her fork down—"that her hands are like claws. Like claws," she repeated, "from work. And she's still living in a sod dugout after six years in Nebraska."

"Claws!" I said, and then ducked my head. Ma stared at me, reminding me that when grown-ups talked, children listened. I couldn't swallow the peas in my mouth. I took a gulp of milk and choked. Billy got up and thumped me on the back.

When I finally got settled down, Pa said, "That's Seth and Millie. I've got more experience farming, and we're younger—"

"What does being young have to do with it!" Grandpa threw his napkin onto the table. "It's still a risk. There's Indians out there, Walter, and wild animals, and winters so cold you can freeze going out to feed the stock."

Freeze! I sunk down in my chair and ran my finger around the edge of the plate. I snuck a glance at Billy. He wasn't grinning anymore.

"Yes, Colonel, I know all that," Pa said impatiently. "There's risks everywhere, in everything we do. Nothing's safe. We weren't safe from the Yankees, we weren't safe from low prices and thieving rascals, we weren't—"

"Hush!" Ma set her fork neatly in the middle of her plate. "That's enough, now. It's bad enough that we're going"—she choked—"going West. Bad enough that we're leaving all we know and love. I won't have us arguing about it, Walter!"

Pa sat back in his chair. Grandpa blew his nose loudly. This is the first change, I thought—Ma speaking up like she never did before.

"No, dear ones, you're right." Grandpa sighed. "We mustn't argue. Too much has happened to us for us to fight. It's just . . ." He stopped.

Ma jumped up, ran over, and put her arms around him. "I know, Papa, I know."

Billy put his fork and knife in the middle of the plate, the way we'd been taught. "Well, I will like living in a sod dugout. Then I won't have to take so many baths."

Ma looked up, her face streaked with tears. "Oh, William, you bad boy. You'll still have to take baths up North."

Suddenly, everyone was laughing. I felt like someone had shut a door in my face and I could never get through it again.

CHAPTER FIVE

"Two axes," Grandpa called out.

"Two axes." I checked where Pa had stored them under the wagon seat.

"One saw." Grandpa held a long list in his hand that fluttered in the cold breeze. He said I was his "supply soldier" and had to check everything inside the wagon.

"One saw." I touched its ragged edge carefully.

"Wrap it!" Grandpa snapped, handing me an old paper. I wrapped the saw and almost saluted.

"One barrel of salt pork."

"One barrel."

"Push it tight against the wagon bows, Sam. The road'll jolt it. I don't want that barrel falling on . . ." He coughed and stared at his list.

Pa would say he was being as melancholy as that old Abe Lincoln. I did hate to see Grandpa worrying; it made me more nervous about leaving. I checked the canvas top; it was pulled down tight and snug. Inside it was like a peddler's wagon, with everything jam-packed into place; baskets and pans hanging from the hickory bows, sacks of food snugged into the corners, all of our bedding folded neatly in the middle, and Ma's chest against one side. My canvas sack was tucked in the corner. Inside was the good-luck stone from Jeb, and Luke's best fishing hook.

"One sack of flour," Grandpa called. I saw the curtains move in the house, and Grandma's white face peered out. Then she frowned, rubbed her eyes, and the curtains swished back.

"One sack and another of apples."

"I'll tell you when to check it, young man! One sack of dried apples," he said loudly.

"One sack." Grandpa sure was grumpy. I knew how he felt.

Billy climbed in beside me and sat on the pile of bedding. His hand was curled up. I made him open it. Inside was a rabbit's foot.

"For luck. I told you before, Harold gave it to me." Billy smiled. "Says it's good for river crossings. 'Powerful across water' is what he says."

I spat out the back of the wagon. "Superstition. Slave superstition!"

Billy tucked his legs under him. "You can say what you like, Sam, but we'll just see when the time comes."

"Bedding!" Grandpa rattled his list.

"I'm sitting on it, Grandpa," Billy said.

Grandpa came and peered in. "Young man, that's not the way to answer. Soldiers answer with one word—'bedding!' "

"But Grandpa, I'm not a soldier. I'm only ten years old." He smiled, and Grandpa reached out and ruffled his hair.

"Besides the bedding," Billy went on, ruining our list, "there's Grandma's dove quilt, which I like a lot. And the wedding chest filled with Ma's herbs and teas. Did you know she has an extra pair of reading glasses, Sam?"

"Mmm." He was so cheerful I wanted to poke him.

"Because she might lose the first pair and 'We'll be in God's forsaken land,' I heard her crying to Grandma last night."

Grandpa cleared his throat. "God does not forsake any land, Billy, remember that. Even if it's wild and cold out there in . . . Dakota Territory . . . God is still there."

"Yes, sir." Even Billy had to salute when Grandpa talked like that. "Wish I could've brought my egg collection, Sam," he whispered.

27

"Those moldy old things?" I straightened my jacket. "It's a good thing we had to leave them behind."

"Oh?" He gave me a wicked little grin. "Just like leaving your bed behind, Samuel T. White?"

"That's different! Pa said we didn't have enough room for two beds, anyone can see that!" But I wished we had room for my bed. Now Billy and I'd have to sleep together, Pa said. It wasn't fair.

"Wish we could take Ma's organ," Billy sang to himself. "Miss that organ, I will, miss those hymns Ma sang."

"I won't miss it," I whispered back. Didn't want Grandpa to hear me. I hated those hymns with valleys of shadows and people bursting up to heaven and all. Didn't make sense.

"You'll miss it when we're out on the lonesome prairie," Billy sang, "and you'll wish we had Ma's organ then." I was about to grab his arm when the house door shot open. Pa leaped down the steps to the muddy drive. He clapped Grandpa on the shoulder. "Ready, Colonel?"

"Ready, son. Reckon there's not much else you can fit in there." Grandpa's voice wasn't as loud as it usually was.

Ma came to the open door, tying a scarf around her new green hat and settling her coat on her shoulders. Her face was white, and her hands fumbled at the scarf. She hesitated for a moment. Pa ran back and helped her down the steps. Grandma followed, apron fluttering.

They all gathered on the drive. Harold had walked up from his house and stood in back of Grandpa. I turned away from him. I didn't want to look too close at someone who said I had "eyes like a hawk and ears like rocks." It was bad luck. A cold, wet wind blew. Somewhere a dove called. Pa stared at the river and his lips moved.

"Ellen, time to go." Carefully, he helped her up onto the driver's seat.

"Get in back, you rascals!" He grinned at us, and we hopped in. Ham and Duke, the two big workhorses Pa bought for the journey, twitched their ears. He'd had to trade Justin for the pair. Grandpa said he should get oxen, but Pa said he never did like oxen, and horses were fine, as long as you didn't push them too hard.

No one said anything. Grandpa tugged on his beard, and Grandma's face screwed up. Suddenly, she ran forward and grabbed Ma's hand. "Good-bye, honey, good-bye. Now, don't work too hard." She glared at Pa. "Keep your bonnet on so the sun won't burn you. Take that camomile tea I gave you and make sure those heathens of yours go to church, *if* there is a church, which I very much doubt." She began to cry and ran around to the back of the wagon.

I leaned out and put my arms around her neck. It felt thin and small.

"Bye, Grandma. I'll miss you." I smelled apples on her shawl. It made me want to cry, thinking of Grandma in the kitchen with her fresh pies and us not there to eat them.

She sniffed and kissed me, then took Billy's face between her two hands and shook it gently. "Behave yourself, William, and remember your grandma, who loves you." Billy kissed her hard. She sort of choked and ran into the house.

Grandpa reached up and pulled Ma forward. He kissed her quickly and pushed her away. He shook Pa's hand. Suddenly, he climbed up the wheel and got in back with us.

"Colonel! What are you doing?" Pa said.

Grandpa sat on the bedding, his long legs poking up. "I want to see what it's like going West, just for a bit. I'll get out soon. I want to see why you're leaving all this behind."

Pa flapped the reins, and we were off. *Clink, jangle-jangle.* Harold waved once and smiled. Billy leaned out and waved at him for a long time. I didn't. I kept touching the fossil stone Jeb gave me, but it didn't make me feel any better. We went down the muddy drive, the dogs barking alongside. Out on the road, past the maple we always climbed. Past the swimming

30

hole and the small brick schoolhouse. At least I wasn't inside, sweating over a slate.

Grandpa peered out the back of the wagon and snorted. "It's like looking through a telescope."

"What do you mean, Grandpa?" I said.

"It's a small, round look at the world." Then I saw what he meant. The white puckers of the wagon cover circled around a picture: one house, a piece of river, one tree, and a cloud.

"Huh! This is the future?" He climbed out the back and jumped down. "Good-bye." His voice was strong, almost angry. Then softer, "Good luck, dear ones, good luck." He whistled to the dogs and they bounded at his heels.

"Good-bye, Jake," I yelled. My eyes watered. I rubbed them hard. Billy stroked his rabbit's foot and blew his nose.

Suddenly he whistled. "Jake! Jake, come with us!"

"William!" Ma said. "You know we agreed not to take any of the dogs. Hush, now!"

But Billy leaned out the back, calling to the dog. Jake stopped in the road, nuzzled Grandpa's knee, and whined. He turned toward Billy and stretched out his long, yellow body. Grandpa stared back at us, his face solemn and tight. Then he pointed, said, "Go!" and Jake bounded toward the wagon. In one great leap, he tried to get in the wagon back and slipped down. Billy and I leaned out to catch him, but we missed.

"Well, boys," Pa said, "if Jake's coming with us, he can't ride in the wagon."

"Oh, Pa." Billy hung out the back.

"Not to start with, anyway," Pa said, and chuckled.

Ma gave an exasperated sigh. "Oh, I guess I am glad that hound dog is coming with us. Life just doesn't seem right somehow without a dog."

Grandpa waved again, and I waved back. My eyes blurred. He turned and walked away from us, fast and hard. His back was straight as a gun.

"Well, you all," Pa said, "we're on our way West!" He whistled, high and shrill, Jake barked, the horses danced sideways, and Ma put her hand to her chest.

CHAPTER SIX

THE WAGON TURNED A CORNER. I leaned out and saw the last bit of Grandpa—his straight back and gray coat. Jake whined and trotted after us.

A mournful whistle came from the front seat.

"Walter!" Ma jerked her coat tight around her shoulders. "Stop that dreadful sound, please! It sounds like a funeral."

I looked over at Billy. He sat hunched against the pork barrel, running his fingers over the rabbit's foot. He sighed.

"I'll miss Grandma." He sniffed and rubbed his nose.

"Crying!"

"Am not." He blew his nose on the corner of his sleeve.

"William!" Ma handed a hankie into the back and gave him such a look. "Just because we're going West doesn't mean you can behave like a savage."

"But Ma, Harold says the Indians aren't savages, that they aren't near what people say they—"

"And what does Harold know about Indians, I'd like to know?" Ma interrupted.

"Exactly." I nudged him. He was stuck. He couldn't say "I was teaching the man to read," because Ma wouldn't like that. He rubbed his nose a third time and sat back against the barrel.

"And don't rub your nose, please!" Ma said, and faced the road.

"Grumpy!" Billy mouthed at me. "She sure is grumpy!"

"Of course she's grumpy!" I hissed. "Leaving her pa and ma, leaving the farm where she grew up. . . ." Suddenly, I felt like putting my arm around Ma and protecting her from everything ahead of us.

Then Billy smiled—a lopsided smile. "She's not any sadder than me, Sam."

Maybe he was smarter than I thought. At least he knew enough to be sad.

I couldn't talk for a bit. My throat was all scratchy, and I kept remembering Pa leaping off on Justin, saying, "Find the future!" If this was finding the future, I didn't want any part of it. I rubbed Jeb's fossil stone for good luck, spat out the back, and watched the road dwindle away.

———————

AT NOON, WE STOPPED IN A WET, BROWN FIELD for lunch. Ma gave us white bread and bacon sandwiches, and Pa uncorked Grandma's stoneware jug and handed it around. Jake lay by the wagon and guarded it.

Billy took a sip. "Lemonade!"

It tasted so good, that sweet-sour drink, with the smoky bacon from Grandpa's pig. Ma held on to the jug for a while, smiling a little. "Reminds me of the picnics we used to take, by the river. . . ."

Pa looked at her and she said quickly, "But I mustn't be looking backward—" She took up the tin dishes and I went with her to a little stream nearby. We crouched on the bank and dipped the dishes in.

"Don't worry, Ma, maybe it won't be so bad. Jeb said as how people are getting rich out West, how there's lots of opportunity—"

"Not you, too, Sam! I thought you'd understand. Women don't want opportunity. They want family and safe homes and gardens and friends living just down the road." She wiped the dishes rapidly and hurried back to the wagon.

I felt foolish. I *knew* how she felt. I'd meant to help take care of her, and I'd just made her angry. I kicked some grass and watched Pa hold out his hand so she could climb up on the wagon. She grabbed hold of the wagon seat and pulled herself up so fast, Pa's mouth dropped open. He jumped after her, told us to get in, and slapped the reins hard.

I didn't like it. I wondered if going West meant they would be scratchy with each other.

"I like that bay horse." Billy sat beside me. "He's got a good nature."

"How d'you know?" I held the stone in my hand before throwing it onto the mattress. If the side with the little white lines came up on top, then we'd get to Dakota Territory safe. If it came up brown, then we'd have trouble. I threw. The white lines spun and settled. I breathed out.

"And you say Harold is superstitious," Billy chuckled. "You can tell by the nose, Sam. Every animal I've ever known that had a bad nature had a crooked nose. Remember that cat, Al? Whew!"

I laughed. "Wasn't he just the devil. Clawed Ma, ran up that tree, spat at Grandpa's bugle. . . ."

"I know how he felt!" Billy grinned. "That's one thing I won't miss—that bugle!"

Pa turned and started to say something. Ma looked straight ahead, her back as stiff as one of those wooden forms dressmakers use. He closed his mouth and snapped the reins again. I could tell by his back he

—

wouldn't miss that bugle, either. I never knew backs could tell so much.

Pa said, "But you're right, Billy. I've noticed the same thing about animals. I like Duke—the bay horse. What do you think about Ham?"

Ham was the roan, a big, hunched horse with shoulders taller than Pa's head. He scared me, his feet big as dinner plates.

"Don't know about him, Pa." Billy sucked on the inside of his cheek. "He's got a bad nose. I'd watch him if I were you."

It reminded me of the way Pa talked to his friends. Suddenly, I felt left out and cold. It began to rain, pattering on the canvas top. Ma got in back with us and handed Pa his black oilcloth coat.

"Thank you, Ellen." He shrugged it on and planted the hat on his head. The rain came harder. Jake kept close to the shelter of the wagon back. The horses lowered their heads, and Pa began to sing "Oh, Susannah." Ma didn't sing, but Billy joined in on the refrain, "Oh, don't you cry for me." When I looked up, I saw her face was wet.

CHAPTER SEVEN

"LOOK AT THAT!" Billy pointed to a broad, flat ferry coming from the far end of the river back to ours. Men sang and pulled on their oars. The ferry came back empty after leaving a wagon on the far side.

"That river's like a big, brown snake." I rubbed my good-luck stone. We'd have to get across it somehow. It was our first big river in the three weeks we'd been traveling northwest since leaving home.

The Mississippi wound back and forth across the wet, brown land. Shabby houses crowded up along its banks. It smelled. Steamboats chugged downriver, barges hauled coal and grain, and people shouted and banged things.

"The old Mississippi," Pa sang, and lit a cheroot. "We could almost swim the wagon across it." He looked at Ham and Duke, measuring their shoulders and strength.

I made the fossil stone jump. Swim! With winter melt in the water?

"Walter." Ma smoothed her hair. "It will be hard enough for the horses just on their own, don't you think?"

"Mmm." Pa sucked in a bunch of smoke and let it out in a long, gray stream.

I breathed out. Ma knew how to talk to him. Nothing sharp or bossy, just a quiet word about the animals.

"Mmm." Pa blew out the last of the smoke in a small ring. We watched it float into the gray sky and disappear. It was so big and wide, and we were rolling along underneath it—free. I poked Billy. He poked me back. We threw each other on the mattress and wrestled.

"Boys, boys!" Ma reproved.

"But, Ma, we're not fighting," Billy said, his face all squished up under me. "We're just . . . practicing."

"That's right, Ma." I pretended to bounce Billy's head. "Just practicing."

I let him up. He grinned at me and hopped down by the horses. I followed.

I took Ham's bridle, Billy grabbed hold of Duke's, and we led them to the ferry landing. There were already three wagons before us, and the sun was just coming up. The wagon in front of us was fine and new. The owner, a man with a beet face, black mustache, and red hat, drove his team of two big oxen nearer the landing. A colt was tied to the back of the wagon—a nice roan with a long tail. He kept dancing at the end of his rope and curving his neck. I got down to look at him.

"Pretty horse," I said to the boy sitting in back of the wagon.

He nodded. "Pa bought it to ride when we get to Oregon."

"Oregon! That's a long way."

"That's what Ma says," he laughed. "Where're you folks going?" He looked about my age, with bat ears and black hair.

"Dakota Territory. Pa says the soil's six feet deep out there. Crops just about grow up overnight." I couldn't help boasting a little. Any fool could see that Pa had made a better choice than this boy's father. Oregon!

"Well, you can't believe everything you hear," the boy said, and munched on an apple.

Billy jumped down beside me. "When our pa says it, you can believe it!"

"Boys, boys," Ma said. "We're all going to better land. Oregon's meant to be very pretty."

The woman in the wagon joined her boy in the back and said, "Apples big as a baby's head, my husband says. And no winter!"

"Apples big as—!" Then I remembered my manners and shut my mouth.

But the boy heard me and clenched his fists. Well, he didn't believe Pa, and I just didn't believe his ma.

"That's fine," Ma said too heartily. When the lady drew her head back into the wagon, Ma muttered, "Missourian talk! Baby's head, indeed!"

Pa chuckled. "Now, Ellen."

I thought, I bet we'll hear talk a lot worse than that before we get to Dakota Territory! I felt kind of sorry for Ma. She sat on that wagon seat like she was sitting on our front porch, all set to receive callers. I bet we wouldn't have a front porch where we were going.

"Get up!" The wagon in front lurched forward, the man driving his oxen with a stick. He shouted and got even redder as he prodded and poked them up to the ferry. You could tell he didn't know anything about animals. Once he was near the ferry, he unhitched his oxen and the colt tied to the back.

"Get down and hold him, will you!" he shouted to his son.

The colt pranced and shied as the men pushed the wagon onto the ferry and blocked its wheels.

"That animal's not broke yet," I said to Billy. "Look at it, will you?"

Pa gripped the reins tighter and leaned forward.

The colt kept pulling and backing with the boy hanging on for dear life. Billy said fiercely, "That poor thing. All scared like that, why I'd like to—"

I never heard what he'd like to do. The man shouted, ran back to the colt, and tied a rope around its neck. "You gotta show him who's boss!" he yelled at his son, and the horse shied again. Billy and I gasped. The boy's face was redder than the man's hat, and he kept patting the animal's neck. I'm glad Pa never made me look foolish in front of strangers that way. He kept shouting as he got on the ferry, towing his son after him.

The ferry moved away from us. The man in the red hat squatted near the back, holding on to the ropes tied to his oxen's horns. His boy knelt beside him, holding on to the lead around the colt's neck. After the animal reared back, the motion of the ferry pulled him into the water and he fought it, hard. Those big, dumb oxen just walked into the river and began to swim. In the middle of the river the current looked wilder and swifter. The ferry men pulled harder on their oars, and suddenly, the boat slewed sideways. The colt struggled to keep up, its nostrils wide and blowing. The oxen were stronger and didn't seem to mind.

"That horse is too scared to swim!" Billy took out his rabbit's foot and rubbed it.

Pa rose from the wagon seat. "That man doesn't know the first thing about horses. If he isn't careful, there'll be real trouble."

The boy hung on to the lead, talking to the animal. I could see how wide and white its eyes were even from where I stood. The ferry lurched again; the colt screamed and tore loose from the boy. Its blazed face stuck out of the water as it headed back toward us.

Pa swore, and Billy grabbed my arm. "Please let him get back, please, God, let the horse swim home." He kissed his rabbit's foot.

Ma grabbed Pa's shoulder. "That poor animal. Isn't there anything we can do, Walter?"

"No, Ellen, that horse is on its own." He shaded his eyes and then said, "Oh!"

The head went under, came up for a second, then went under again. Billy and I jumped up beside Ma and Pa on the wagon seat to see better. "Come on, horse!" Billy shouted. "Come up!"

People yelled on the ferry. The husband tried to jump into the river—to help the colt, I guess—but the wife wasn't having any of it. She dragged on his arm and screeched, and finally the man threw down his hat and stomped on it. He shouted something to his boy, who threw a looped rope out to the place the colt went under.

The rope trailed in the current. The colt was gone. I tried not to see it, but my mind kept making pictures. I saw the colt sinking to the bottom, its lungs filling up with water; I felt it thinking of the warm sun and the wind and how good the grass felt when it rolled, and it tried to get up from the river bottom, and it just couldn't, it was so tired. And maybe it was tired of getting yelled at and being hauled around by that loud man in the red hat. Billy blew his nose and let go of my arm.

"God, that river!" he swore.

"Billy!" Ma swatted his ear. "Don't you swear!" She dabbed her nose and said, "Somehow it's worse, Walter, that it was a colt. So pretty and young."

Pa's knuckles were white. "That man was a fool, Ellen! Anyone could see that animal was barely halter broke. Taking it all the way to Oregon!" His cheeks were red above his beard. He even sounded angry with us. "Get in back, boys. Hurry up now!"

"Powerful against water," I said as we crawled in back.

He almost punched me. "It only works for who's carrying it, Sam!"

"Boys, boys," Ma soothed.

It would take more than that to soothe me. That whole family was foolish, from the mother with her "low" words, to the father shouting and carrying on, to that boy. A soldier wouldn't have allowed that horse to drown.

When the ferry came back for us, Pa got down and unhitched the horses. Billy and I held them while Pa and the men pushed the wagon onto the ferry and blocked the wheels.

"Sam, you grab this rope." He tied one around Duke's neck, and he took hold of Ham's rope.

"Jake's coming with us, isn't he, Pa?" Billy patted the dog's head.

"Of course. I wouldn't make him swim the Mississippi."

Billy held out his hand and, keeping close to Billy's knees, Jake followed him onto the ferry.

We all got on the ferry, and it began to move. Jake whined and slunk under the wagon. Duke's brown neck rippled. He stomped his feet. "There, boy, there. Come on," I called, pulling on the lead. He hesitated at the river's edge, and stepped in.

"Get up, Ham!" Pa coaxed, and tugged on the rope. Ham shied, pulled back, and then plunged into the water, swimming beside Duke.

"They'll be all right, Sam." Pa looked at me. "They're good, strong horses—not like that colt. Don't you boys worry. Hold on to that lead to keep Duke steady, Sam."

"You try this time." Billy handed me his rabbit's

foot. The freckles stood out on his face like mud spatters.

I kept the rope in my left hand and gave him the fossil stone. We both worked on those good-luck charms, saying prayers under our breath. The boat creaked when we got to the middle of the river. The ferry slipped sideways, and I gripped Duke's lead tighter. The horses were swimming strongly behind us, but you never knew. That colt went under in a second.

Pa was talking over his shoulder to the ferrymen, but I didn't really hear him. It seemed as if there was just Billy and me, the horses, the boat and the river, and our words and fingers on the good-luck charms keeping us safe. Finally, the ferry touched land. Ma sighed. "Well, here we are. Here we are."

Pa and I ran up onto the bank, pulling on the leads. Ham snorted and splashed his way out of the water, getting me all wet. Good old Duke just stepped onto land like a lady out of her bath. The men pushed the wagon off the ferry, and Pa hitched up again. Billy handed me a towel to get dry.

"Here's your rabbit's foot." I handed it over. "Worked better this time."

He nodded and rubbed his nose. "Poor colt. No more grass. No more rolls in the morning. No more gallops in the field."

I felt like a friend died. We sat in back of the wagon with our knees pulled up to our chests.

"No more looking at the moon," I said.

"No more stars overhead."

"No more grain in a bucket."

"No more cold water on a hot afternoon."

Then we were quiet. Ma got back up onto the wagon seat, after paying that greasy ferryman. Pa clucked to Ham and Duke and we started off.

Billy spat out the back. "Murdering old Mississippi."

"Murdering old Mississippi," I whispered, and spat. The wagon jounced, Billy leaned against me, and I didn't move away.

CHAPTER EIGHT

WIND DROVE THE RAIN AGAINST THE CANVAS top. Billy, Ma, and I huddled close together in back, wrapped in our blue wool coats and Grandma's quilt. Pa drove, looking like a stuffed scarecrow with all his jackets and his oilcloth coat on. Poor Ham and Duke plodded ahead, their heads low and unhappy. Jake trotted behind the wagon, his coat plastered and wet.

"It'll get better soon," Pa said, without turning around.

"When's soon?" I wanted to know.

"Hush." Ma did not smile. "Don't sass your pa. Soon is when . . . soon is." She didn't finish, pulling the quilt tighter around her shoulders.

"Soon is when spring comes," Billy sang, "soon is when the rain stops, soon is when the sun comes out. Right, Pa?"

"That's right, son." Pa smiled at him. It was a strange thing, but Pa didn't seem to have any of his dark days now, though it sure was dark outside.

"Bound to get better," Ma said firmly, more to herself than to us, I think. "It can't rain *every* day, can it, Walter?"

"No, Ellie, it can't. Didn't that guidebook say 'scorching blue skies and sun'? They can't lie in those books. People have gone before us on this route, and they know. 'Course, we're still only in Missouri. We're not West yet."

Billy looked at me. We were beginning to doubt that old guidebook. Billy pretended to write, and wobbled his head like a silly person with no brains. I laughed, and choked when Ma gave me a stern look.

"Poor horse," Billy whispered. "All dead on the bottom of the river. Ma? Where will that horse wind up? On a bank somewhere?"

"William, don't be morbid!"

"What's 'morbid,' Ma?"

"Thinking too much about the sad, hard things in life." Ma wiped a drip on the end of her nose and shivered. "It's time to stop thinking about that colt, William. That was yesterday."

Billy's words got me thinking. I saw that poor old colt swept along by the current, turning over and over underwater, snagging himself on a branch somewhere. And maybe some boy would be walking along the riverbank someday and he'd look down, fishing maybe, and see this *nose* coming up out of the water, only maybe it wouldn't look like a nose because it had been in the water so long. . . .

"Sam, are you all right?" Ma peered at me.

"What's that?" I shook myself. I felt queasy.

"You moaned, Sam," Billy said.

"I was thinking about that horse—that colt." Billy pulled up his collar.

I clenched my fists. "It makes me so mad that we couldn't do anything—that that stupid man just let it get swept away. Why, if he'd only—"

"Hush, Sam!" Pa said. "There's nothing we can do about it now. What's gone is gone."

I just pulled my legs up to my chest and felt miserabler and miserabler. Even the thought of Jake trotting behind didn't help.

The wheels sucked in mud, and Billy swayed against me. I put my head on my knees and almost cried. Losing that colt felt like all I'd left behind—Grandma and Grandpa and our safe, warm house.

"Sam." Billy nudged me. "Sam? How about we have a funeral service for that colt? Would that make it better?" His eyes gleamed.

I raised my head. "But we can't bury him, not the way we did Al or that pig of yours." Billy was probably the only person in the world to have a funeral for a pig, his little pig, Eleanor. She died of a cold, and we buried her near the linden tree with flowers, and Billy had Harold come play the penny whistle for Eleanor.

"I know that. But you can still have a service, can't you, Ma?"

"Of course, boys, if it will make you feel better, you do just that." She smiled gently.

"When we stop, Sam, we'll do it then."

TOWARD DUSK, PA GAVE OUT A SHOUT.

"What, Walter?" Ma sounded afraid. She'd been mentioning Indians from time to time, and each time she said the word, her voice shivered.

Pa shouted again. "Wagons ahead!"

Billy and I crowded up behind the driver's seat. Poor old Ham and Duke looked just about gone, sweat darkening their backs, their haunches black with rain. Ahead, through the wet, I saw flickering lights, shapes moving around it, and some wagons beside.

"Walter?" Ma grabbed his shoulder. "You sure it's—our kind of people? Not—Indians?"

" 'Course I'm sure, Ellie. Indians don't have wagons, and that sure is a wagon over there." He slapped the reins, and Ham and Duke shambled into a trot.

Billy bounced on the mattress. "A fire, Sam! People to talk to! Oh, boy!"

I was excited myself. Somebody else besides just us, some new talk. Maybe there'd be someone my own age. Somebody to go fishing with or set a snare for a rabbit with.

We jounced to a stop and Pa swung down. He dried Jake with a rag and told him to stay under the wagon. Billy and I tethered the horses. I wiped down Duke, while Billy took care of Ham. He'd struck up a friendship with that bad-nosed horse by bribing him with grain. Ma stayed in the wagon. "Until we know who's here, Walter."

Pa gave her a look and said, "This isn't the front porch of your house anymore, Ellie. Who's here is who's here."

Ma hesitated a moment and then climbed down into Pa's waiting arms.

"Hey, the rain's stopped!" Billy held out both hands. "Look!" He pointed to a sky where the wind blew the clouds away in great, ragged wisps. Tiny, black birds flew overhead, swooping and fluttering. A pale sun lit on the wet, muddy ground. Ahead were five wagons. Oxen stomped their big, splayed feet and nuzzled the earth. Three kids in muddy clothes darted underneath the wagons.

"Can't catch me!" "Can!" "Can't!"

Some women and older girls bent over the camp-fires, stirring things. Two dogs whined nearby, waiting for scraps. The men were busy wiping down the oxen or repairing the axles and tongues of their wagons.

"What a road, eh?" Pa said to the nearest man. "I'm Walter White, from Kentucky, going north to Dakota Territory. Where are you folks going?"

"Nebraska," said one man with a skinny red beard.

"California," said another man with a hat pulled low over his eyes.

"Depends on who you ask," one of the women called out to us. "We're kind of making it up as we go along." She laughed, a great big horsebelly of a laugh. Billy looked at me, and I could tell what he was thinking: I'm glad Ma's laugh isn't like that!

Ma swept by us up to the campfire and put out her hand. "I'm Ellen White, from Kentucky. My, I'm glad to see another woman traveling."

"Isn't it just the thing," a stout woman in a smeary apron said, and she and Ma commenced to talk. About traveling, keeping linens dry, keeping children clean and dry, trying to make fires in the rain, about stores and jellies and oxen's feet and all.

I went over to one of the boys who was leaning against a wagon tongue. "Hi. I'm Sam White."

"From Kentucky, I hear." The boy spat to the side.

"What's wrong with Kentucky?" I flared up.

"Why, nothing, nothing at all. We're from Tennessee. We're all Southerners here."

Thank God for that. Billy came and stood by my side. I was surprised; he usually was so forward and not shy or anything. Maybe he was thinking about the colt.

"This is my brother, Billy." We nodded at each other, and another boy came out of the shadows.

"How do you like going west—or north, wherever it is we're all going?" he laughed.

I liked him right away. Looked a bit like a snipe, with a long, skinny nose, thin legs, and his head kind of bobbed forward when he spoke. His brown eyes were friendly.

"I like it—some," I said. "Mostly I like not being in school."

"Me, too!" the boy said. "I'm Allan. Allan Grant. I sure don't miss those squeaky slates!"

"Me, neither! Maybe we won't have to go to school where we're going. We'll have too much work to do." I felt cheerful all of a sudden. "We'll be too far from town to have a school."

"Maybe," said the first, dark boy, whose name was Harry. "But you know how mothers are. They got schooling on the brain. They see it in the sky.

They see it in the trees, the road, everywhere they look. 'Why, Harry,' they'll say. 'Tell me what kind of cloud that is. Didn't Alfred Lord Tennyson write a poem about clouds?' "

I guess neither Billy nor I felt much like laughing. We still had something to do. Billy tugged on my sleeve. "Sam? If we're going to do it, we'd better do it now."

"We have to do something for . . . for our folks," I explained to the boys. "We'll be back soon."

Billy and I ran behind our wagon. There wasn't any other place we could be alone, with no trees or woods around.

"Here," Billy knelt down by the big, muddy wheel and got out his knife.

"You'll ruin it, Billy."

"Hush!" He dug in the dirt, making a small hole. I crouched beside it.

Billy looked up at the sky and said, "Into this hole, we put the spirit of that red colt."

"Roan colt," I whispered.

"Roan colt. We put here his long legs."

"His long legs," I repeated.

"His sweet coat."

"His sweet coat."

"His nice nose."

"Nose."

"His long tail."

I couldn't talk then, seeing that horse and all of its beautiful parts gone forever.

Billy sighed, spat into the hole, and looked at me. I wiped my eyes and spat. He pushed dirt over the hole. "Good-bye, horse."

"He needs a name," I whispered.

Billy nodded.

"How about—Hank?" I said.

"Good-bye, Hank," Billy said. "Run wild some-place else besides this earth."

"In a place with no loud men in red hats." I patted the ground.

I stood, and Billy stood beside me. His face was solemn and quiet. We put our hands out and touched over the colt's grave.

CHAPTER NINE

Billy's shoulder touched mine. We sat side by side on a log near the fire. The men smoked and told stories about river crossings and how far they'd come.

"That Mississippi. Reach out and grab you if it could," the man with the red beard said. "It's a mean old river."

His wife murmured something about a "mean old country, from start to finish," but the man ignored her. Some other ladies nodded and pursed their lips.

Allan sat beside me. "What will you do once you get to Dakota Territory?"

"Work, I guess. Help Pa plow the fields and plant—take care of stock—if we get stock."

"Help build the dugout," Billy said, digging in the mud with a stick. He was being pretty quiet—for Billy. Maybe he was still sad about Hank.

"That's heavy work," Allan said. "Plowing up the prairie, cutting it into bricks—least, that's what Pa says."

"When Pa does it, it won't be so heavy," Billy said firmly. "Pa knows how to do things."

He sure was certain about that. I guessed Pa knew. I *hoped* he knew.

"You'll be up North," Harry said, spitting beyond into the dark. An ox stomped and blew through his nose.

"I know that," I said. "Pa says that doesn't matter anymore."

Harry spat again, and I clenched my fists.

"If Pa says it doesn't matter"—Billy stood—"then it won't. He fought in the war. He says it's dead and gone." He disappeared behind me. I didn't see where he went.

"Well," Allan said, "it's bound to be different, wherever we're all going. New territory, new people."

"I like old territory," I whispered. "I like old people."

We listened to a man play a violin. They sang "Old Dan Tucker," and one man got up and danced near the fire. People began to clap.

Ma beckoned to me. I followed her to the wagon.

"It's bedtime, Sam. Where's William?"

"I don't know. He disappeared."

"You check inside, then."

I climbed into the back, and Billy was curled asleep on our mattress. He was holding tight to the rabbit's foot, and his face looked awful young.

"There." Ma drew up the covers. "It's been a long day. Seeing all these people is tiring. Don't know how it is, but I'd forgotten how noisy people are."

Pa climbed into the wagon, they blew out the light, and we curled up. The canvas walls let every sound through. A man coughing and spitting. A baby fretting. Someone arguing. The violin changed from dance tunes to old, sad ones about leaving home. I put my face against Billy's shoulder, and all I could see behind my eyelids was Grandpa walking away from us.

———————————

"A SUNBONNET." Ma held up the pattern for Pa to admire. "See, Walter, how the back frill protects your neck, and the front panels protect your cheeks." She sighed and laid the pattern in the wagon back the next morning.

Billy put his hands to the side of his face. "Can't see a thing, Ma. I don't know how you stand it."

"Will stand it," Ma said firmly. "I'm not used to them yet, but I soon will be."

—

Pa and I finished hitching up Ham and Duke and got in the wagon. "That rest did them good, Ellie. Even a day here in camp helped. Horses aren't like oxen, thank goodness. You have to rest them a bit more."

Ma smiled. Ever since she'd met Mrs. Wilson, who gave her the sunbonnet pattern, and Mrs. Grant with her baby, she'd been more cheerful—more like her old self. Didn't scold as much.

"Water in the buckets, William?" Pa said. That was his chore, to fill the buckets that hung under the wagon back.

" 'Course, Pa." Billy unbuttoned the top of his coat. Looked like it was getting tighter to me. He must be growing. It wasn't fair. He couldn't be getting bigger than me! I held out my arms.

"Ma? Do you think I'll ever grow?" They looked the same to me.

"Of course, Sam, you're bound to grow. Grandpa didn't get his height till he was eighteen."

Eighteen! That was centuries away. People might see Billy and say, "Oh, so you're the older one, and Sam, here, must be the *younger* one." I couldn't stand that!

"Ma?" Billy said. "Could I ride in the Laskers' wagon? Just for a change?" Pa'd already told us that two wagons—the Laskers' and the Smiths'—would be traveling with us for a while. The Grants and Allan were going on another road.

"All right, William, but you come back with us when we stop for lunch."

Billy bounded off, and we saw him starting to climb the back of the Laskers' wagon. I was glad to see him go for a bit—Mr. Growing William.

Ma waved to her friend. "Good-bye, Cecelia, good-bye. You be careful, now, and stay out of that western sun. California's awful sunny."

"You be careful, too," Mrs. Wilson called back. Her face was purple as a plum. It was clear she wasn't staying out of any sun. "Watch out for those Dakota winters. Hear they're something terrible!"

Ma grinned. I saw her. Not just a smile tipping up the corners of her mouth, but a big, wide grin. Why, at home she'd never give the time of day to a woman like Mrs. Wilson. I guess she was changing. Wasn't sure I liked it. She waved to Mrs. Grant, who was making johnnycakes by the fire, and I waved to Allan.

He shouted, "Good luck!"

"Get up, boys." Pa flapped the reins, and off we went. Jake barked and trotted after us, his eyes eager. I think he liked going West. Across the field we went, rocking up onto the muddy road. The two wagons followed us. Pa and Ma swayed back and forth, touching shoulders. I leaned against a flour sack and watched them. They looked so companionable all of a sudden, touching shoulders. Like partners.

I thought about our crops going into the dark earth, and how we'd be rich once we harvested them. That's what Pa said. Maybe in the fall I'd get a pony and a rifle of my own. Maybe I could even get one of those hunting jackets with the leather patches. Billy would probably want something stupid.

We stopped at noon in a wet field. Pa drove the horses off the road; the other wagons followed. Mr. Lasker jumped down and started a fire, while Mrs. Lasker spread out some plates and food. I walked over.

"Did Billy bother you much talking?"

Mr. Lasker tugged on his red beard. "He didn't bother us, son, because he wasn't with us. I thought he changed his mind and was riding with you." His eyes looked small and weaselly.

I felt cold inside my chest. "Pa?" I ran back to our wagon. "Pa, Billy's not with the Laskers'."

Pa stopped rubbing Duke. "Did you try the other wagon, the Smiths'? He must be with them." He strode along beside me.

"My boy with you?" Pa spoke to Mrs. Smith, who was wiping the nose of her small, fretting child.

"No, Mr. White. I thought he was with the Laskers'." The little boy cried and put his face in her apron.

"That's what we thought, too." Pa sounded grim. He went over to Mr. Lasker, who was busy oiling up his harness.

"If we've lost that boy, you'll have me to speak to, Lasker!" And he strode back to our wagon. He unhitched Duke from his harness and put a bridle on.

"Sam, you take Duke and Jake back along the road and find Billy. I've got to stay here with your mother in case—in case this takes a while." I could just see the other wagons setting off after lunch, leaving Ma all on her own if Pa were with me. We couldn't allow that!

Ma bit her lip. "Where could he be, Walt? He can't be far behind, can he? Probably in camp?" She pushed at her hair and wiped her hands twice on her clean apron. "It's my fault. I should have looked in the Laskers' wagon before we left."

"It's not *your* fault, Ellie." Pa spat to the side, glaring at the Laskers' wagon. "There's some people just not worth the spot of earth they stand on!"

I swung up onto Duke and pulled in the reins. I felt miles above the earth, and my chest was cold and tight. I turned the horse back onto the road and kicked him to a trot. Jake followed. We had to find Billy. Soon.

I bounced along the road, looking on either side. What if Billy was in camp? That was a whole morning away. The wind blew against my back and I turned up my collar. The hat Ma had made for me with warm earflaps was snug and tight. Snug and tight, the way we were at night together in the wagon—Pa and Ma at one end, Billy and I curled against each other nearby.

Duke snorted and slowed to a walk. Jake barked at his heels, almost as if he knew.

"Get up, get up!" I kicked Duke hard. "We have to find William. Hurry!" I looked between Duke's hairy ears at the muddy road. No Billy. Maybe he was holding tight to that rabbit's foot of his, running down the road. Or maybe he got scared and just ran off. He wasn't very smart about practical things. He could have just wandered off in the wrong direction. I'd heard enough stories about children who got lost on the prairie being found frozen stiff as a board days later.

The wind blew harder. I blinked hard. This was awful. This could be the worst thing that ever happened to us since the war, or since the time Grandpa stepped on that rusty nail and was sick for weeks and weeks. If Billy was lost, Grandma would never forgive me. She'd told me to watch out for my brother. And I hadn't watched out. I'd been too busy thinking about how rich we'd be and wanting that dratted hunting jacket and pony.

Suddenly Jake leaped forward, barking. Something bobbed along the horizon. Jake ran toward it, and that black speck got closer. Duke shambled into a canter. "Billy? Billy, that you?" A small blue coat got bigger and bigger. Jake met him and jumped all over him. They ran toward me.

I slid off Duke, holding tight to the reins. Billy ran up and hugged me. "Oh, Sam, am I glad to see you! You can't think how scared I was. I've been walking and running forever!" He put his hands over his face. "I was just about to leave with the Laskers and then I had to find a flower to put on Hank's grave, and all I could find was some new grass. So I put that on his grave, and when I looked up, you were gone!" He sobbed, and Jake nuzzled him and whined.

He wiped his eyes. "And the Wilsons were going, too, and they said to just start on that road and keep going and never stop, but, oh, Sam!"

"Hush, hush, it's all right, Billy. I'm here, Sam's here. I wouldn't leave you. Why, we got just as worried as you when we found out." I hugged him. "You bet Pa'll have some sharp words for Lasker. What a weasel that man is."

Billy sniffed. "He is a bit like a weasel, isn't he?"

"That skinny old red hair," I said.

"Those tiny, beady eyes." Billy blew his nose. "Oh, Sam. I don't think I've ever been so glad to see you before. Ever."

"All right, now. Let's get back to Pa and Ma before they have the cavalry out looking for us. You know how scared Ma is about Indians, though God knows we haven't seen many."

Billy swung up on Duke and I mounted. "You said *God*, Sam."

I kicked Duke and we trotted up the road. "I guess I can say it if I want to when we're alone."

Billy held me tight around the waist. He didn't say anything more until we got to the field with Pa's wagon.

Pa and Ma ran up to us, and Pa pulled Billy down from the horse. He looked at him, panting, his beard wild.

"William"—Pa sucked in a breath—"I don't know if I should whip you or kiss you."

"Kiss me," Billy said, and burst into tears again.

CHAPTER TEN

THE LAND WAS CHANGING. The smaller hills and red rocks of the South were gone, and day by day, the land got more and more like a blanket—a brown-green, rumpled one. Grandma'd want to pull it neat and flat, but I liked it. Like the sea was supposed to be, and sometimes I felt we were on a boat sailing over an ocean.

We went over so many miles of grass, it all began to look the same. We got quieter the farther north we traveled. Sometimes the only sound I heard was the wind flapping our canvas top. Something about that wide blue sky, that endless grass, made us quiet. Like our voices were a fire we had to save.

After a few weeks of rolling over the new grass, Pa turned to us. "We're in Dakota Territory now. We got here!"

Billy said, "Looks just the same to me, Pa. Grass and grass and sky and wind."

Pa frowned.

"I like it, Pa," Billy hurried to say. "It's just it doesn't look any different."

Ma patted his arm and I silently agreed. I wondered if she was thinking about living in the ground, the way Pa said we would. Dig into a hill with the wind at our backs, he said. I wondered if it would feel like a grave instead of a house, but I didn't tell Billy that.

After another week, we came to the first town we'd seen in some time.

"What's that?" Billy asked.

You could hardly tell it was a town at first. There were just some bumpy bits on the horizon. Then, as the wagon rolled on, they became house roofs, then walls, and a dusty street snaked between them.

Pa stopped Ham and Duke outside the town, and Ma fidgeted with her handkerchief. She dabbed at her cheeks and hands, and pushed her straggly hair under the dusty bonnet.

"Walter, do I look all right?"

"You always look lovely, Ellen," Pa said.

She shook her head. "Bonnets are no use in this country—all that wind and sun." She "tcched." "You boys smooth down your hair and neaten up."

Billy stared at me and I stared at him. I straightened his dusty jacket and he brushed off my shoulders and we laughed. Used to be that I'd fuss at him and he'd fuss back. But ever since that time weeks ago when he was almost lost, I'd stopped picking at him quite so much.

Pa chirruped to the horses, and we went into town. There were five or six houses on either side, cows in back, and horses tied in front of the "Comfort Hotel." It was a skinny, gray building like an old lady trying to pretty herself up. Faded pink curtains hung inside the windows, and the glass was smeary.

There were people all over the street, calling and talking to each other. "Harry!" someone shouted, and my ears hurt. "How's your boy? Alice doing well?" "Sure!" the other shouted back. Didn't they know you didn't need to shout on the prairie? That it was so quiet a whisper would do?

The only ones who were quiet were Indians. We'd seen a few on horseback when we traveled, but not many. Here an older man stood straight as a gun by the Comfort Hotel, and a younger one stood beside him. In the shadows crouched a woman. They didn't talk to each other, but the quiet around them seemed to join them up somehow, and we just looked noisy and silly compared to them.

Ma said, "Indians!"

"Hush," Pa said. "They have a right to be here, too. Just go about your business and don't fuss."

"What's that, Pa?" Billy pointed to a long line of men outside a shabby building.

"That's probably the land claim office, Billy, and those men are waiting to file on their claims."

Pa stopped the horses by the general store and said, "You boys can come with us or stay here."

Billy jumped down and went in with Ma and Pa, but I stayed in the wagon. "Come on, Sam." He waved to me.

I shook my head, and couldn't explain to him that there were too many people and too many voices, and I just wasn't used to it. Made my neck itch, and I scrunched down to watch people while Ma and Pa bought supplies. Most folks looked like us, kind of tattered. Nobody was too neat—men had scrungy beards and blue denim overalls. Women were in calico with kids tugging at their hands. One yellow mutt with a sad tail lay in the street.

After a long, noisy time they came back, and Pa heaved a sack of flour into the wagon while Ma tucked a bag beside it.

"Glad I got that map, Ellen," Pa said. Even his voice sounded loud to me.

"Yes, Walter—I was glad to have a little conversation with the storekeeper. News!" Ma said.

"What news?" I asked. "I bet it's still the same. Storms. Woman has five babies. Horses run amok and little boy squashed. Tornadoes in the South and—"

"Railroads, Sam!" Billy broke in. "You forgot the railroads."

"Coming this way," Pa said. "It makes me think. . . ."

"Think what, Walter?" Ma hopped up onto the seat.

"Think that we may be getting near to stopping."

"It would be so wonderful to stop, just to sit for a while. Not to move," Ma sighed.

"The storekeeper drew me a rough map, Ellie, of the territory still open around here. Just in case."

Pa smiled at her, flicked the reins, and we set off down the street. I was so glad to be going again, to get out of that town and beyond all those voices and legs and arms. I didn't know if I wanted to stop moving or not.

"Sam, you should have seen the candy! And guns and knives and fishing poles!"

"Mmmph," was all I said to Billy.

I watched the prairie roll by, and it swept my mind clean—the cool wind and the sky so wide and high. Who wanted to look at candy?

Suddenly, Billy nudged me and pointed out the back. Two hawks dove after a pigeon. They screamed at that bird as it zigzagged and flew low.

"Come on, pigeon!" Billy called. "Fly faster!"

It whizzed to one side, raced to the other, gained height, dove, but the hawks stayed close behind. One of the hawks rose higher and higher, then screamed again. It sped down the sky and hit the pigeon so hard its feathers exploded into the air.

"Whooh! Hate to be that pigeon!" Billy sucked in a breath.

"Me, too." I looked through the back. There was no one out here on the prairie except us—us and those screaming hawks and the pigeon exploded into nothing. The wind blew the feathers away, it blew away the hawks' calls. I shivered and couldn't stop.

———

CHAPTER ELEVEN

A NIGHT AND A DAY AFTER WE LEFT THAT DRAB town, Pa turned to Ma on the wagon seat.

"Ellie, it's about time we thought of making a claim."

"How are we going to choose, Walter?"

Pa stopped and unfolded the map he'd got in town. He ran his finger down the paper. "It's divided into sections, Ellen, and each section is one hundred sixty acres."

Ma studied the map. Pa said, "These are the sections that are still unclaimed. The ones closer to town are already gone. But we could try to find something near the next town—about forty miles away."

"Forty miles!" Ma jumped down from the wagon and dusted off her dress. She looked around and breathed in. To the left, the plain ran up to a little hump, flattened, and stretched out to some hills far away. They were purple and brown, with cloud shadows racing over them. To the right, the grass was brown and green. Birds popped up from it and swung on the stems. Ham and Duke lowered their heads to graze. Jake rolled on his back in the grass.

"What's wrong with this?" Ma said.

"Here? But I thought you wanted neighbors, to be closer to town. The last one's more than a day away."

"I know. I know it's contrary of me, but . . ." She walked back and forth, taking deep breaths. Billy and I jumped down beside her. The ground was springy and soft, and I threw myself on it, rolling and kicking my feet. Earth. Land that didn't move under the wagon wheels.

Billy rolled beside me, and we rootled and snorted like two spring pigs. Jake bounced from my head to Billy's, pretending to snap at us.

"Boys!" Ma reproved. But her mouth twitched.

Pa laughed and jumped down beside us. "If this doesn't beat all." He swung Ma around until her bonnet fell off and her hair streamed out behind.

"Walt! Put me down." He did, and she looked like an Indian woman then, with her brown face and hands and dark hair. Grandma'd hate it. She'd want to stuff Ma's hair under the bonnet and dab cornstarch on her skin.

"Well, boys"—Pa kept his hand on Ma's waist—"what do you think?"

We scrambled to our feet and Billy said, "If there's water nearby, this looks fine to me."

He sure was getting practical all of a sudden. I hadn't even thought of water.

Pa pointed to some trees in the distance. "Those are willows. Should mean a creek over there."

"If this section's free," Ma said, pinning up her hair. "*And* if no one else wants it." She got the map from the wagon, and she and Pa pored over it, murmuring—"That track there—meant to be a road—goes through the middle of these four sections—that pine there. . . ." I guess they were figuring out landmarks. Billy and I lay down in the grass and looked up at the sky while they talked.

"You could fall into it," Billy said.

"Or swim around in it, like a blue sea."

"The air smells good!" He chewed on some grass. "Clean, like laundry."

"Or potatoes baking."

"Mmm, I like it here." Billy rolled onto his side. "Harold would like this, all that open space and—"

"No, he wouldn't," I interrupted. "Harold'd think it was too wild and too cold. He's a slave."

"*Was* a slave." Billy flushed.

"And they can't live with cold the way we can."

"We'll see," Billy said, "we'll just see how you do, Sam, when the snow comes."

I prickled up then and reached over to jab his arm, but he rolled away as Pa yelled to us.

"We're clear, boys!" He ran over and pretended to put his foot on each of our chests. "We declare this to be Walter T. White's—"

"And Ellen A. White's—" Ma put in.

"And Billy and Sam White's land," we all finished together.

Pa rubbed his chin. "Who'll come with me to look for water?"

Billy jumped up and they set off together, singing, while Ma pulled grass out of a circle to make a fire. "Sam, help me get dinner started." Of course Billy *would* get to go exploring while I had to help with supper.

"In a minute, Ma." I did something strange, then, something I never told anyone about, not even Billy. I went off behind the wagon, where no one could see me, and dug a tiny hole with my knife. The grass roots tangled up the dirt and it took a while. I sniffed the wet earth smell. Then I spat into the hole three times and mixed it in, tamping the grass hard on top.

"Samuel, you come here!" Ma's voice rose.

"Coming." I felt strange doing such a thing. But when I saw Pa and Billy running back toward the wagon, waving their hats and shouting, "We found water!" I knew why. I'd put a piece of myself into the earth. Samuel Theodore White, a Kentucky boy, had made his mark on Dakota Territory.

CHAPTER TWELVE

PA LEFT THE NEXT DAY FOR THE CLAIMS OFFICE. "Got to get there quick to get this piece. Wish I'd known we wanted this when we went through town."

"You'll get it, Pa." Billy smiled. "You'll see."

Pa ruffled his hair, jumped into the wagon, and waved. I felt so lone and hollow watching him get smaller and smaller in that grass.

"Come!" Ma tapped me. "Let's get things set up here and we won't feel so lonely without Pa."

We set up a tent from the canvas top, Billy piled stones around a cleared space for the campfire, and I got firewood from the creek. It was a nice creek, deep in places, with tree shadows on the black water. Jake stuck his nose in it and drank long and deep. Fish swam under the banks, and a kingfisher rattled downstream. You always know there's plenty of fish when you see a kingfisher.

When I dumped the firewood by the tent, I heard Billy calling, "Sam!" I ran over to where he was crouched. He pointed to a thick bunch of grass.

"Peep-peep," came from the shadows.

"Prairie chickens," Billy whispered.

A bird stuck her beak out partway and jerked it back. She burst out of the grass, scaring us both. Dragging her wing, she ran peeping away from us.

"She wants us to follow her," I whispered. We walked after her to set her mind at rest.

"I like it here," Billy said quietly. "I like prairie chickens. I like big clouds."

I was quiet. You couldn't argue about whether the clouds were too big or the sky too empty. Billy liked it, and I didn't—not yet. Would I ever get used to it?

I heard Pa before I saw him. The soft thud-thud of Ham's and Duke's hooves on the prairie.

"Billy! Get over here. Pa's coming!" He ran over beside me, and Ma followed. We didn't say anything as we watched him come closer, didn't say to each other, "Do you suppose? Did he get it? What will we do if he didn't?" We didn't ask those questions during the long days of waiting.

The sun glinted on something in the back of the wagon. And that's how I knew we got the land.

"Pa!" I ran toward the wagon and horses. "Pa! You got it!"

He stood up, waved his hat, and whooped. "We got it! It's ours." He clucked the horses to a trot, and they rattled toward us, Pa whooping and waving. A cookstove and the brand-new plow bounced in the back. I could see it was a breaking plow, made just for prairie sod. Pa wouldn't have bought it if the land weren't ours.

"Whoa!" He stopped the horses and jumped down, picking Ma up and whirling her around until her hair flew out behind. Jake barked and leaped beside them.

"Walter!" she protested, and finally he put her down.

"We were lucky we got here when we did. You won't believe it, but this was the last section open!"

Ma patted her hair into a bun. "All the rest are settled up?"

"Yup. We'll have some neighbors. I guess we got the land, though, because some people are still scared of the Indians."

Ma pursed her lips.

"But it's nothing to worry about, Ellie, nothing at all. The fort's thirty miles away, and we were smart to go into north territory."

Then he swooped down on us, hugging Billy and me tight to his rough coat. It smelled like Pa. Tobacco smoke, outdoors, and something I couldn't name. Something fierce and spicy.

Then Pa kissed Ma so loud his lips popped, and she blushed, and I punched Billy, I was so excited. We rolled around on the ground, wrestling, until Ma stopped us.

Safe. We were safe. We got the land from the government, and it was ours as long as we planted ten acres, built a house, and stayed for five years. That didn't sound so hard. No Northerners could come and take it away. We wouldn't look out one day and see our bottom land all shrunk to nothing, the way Grandpa did after the war.

———————

PA TOOK A SHORT NAP, WHILE MA PUT THE wagon to rights, and after lunch he said, "Where do you want your house, sweetheart?"

Ma stood and walked around the campfire. She strolled off toward the creek, paused, and shaded her eyes. Billy ran after, and I followed, Jake at my heels. I wasn't about to let him help pick out a house site without me! She kept walking toward the creek where black willows bent in the wind. A crow lifted from a top branch and flew over us. I spat to one side for good luck. I didn't like crows. Too much like mourners at a funeral.

———

When Ma stopped on top of a small rise, Billy said, "This would be good, Ma. It's right near the stream. Good for winter and carrying water."

She patted his head. "That's my practical boy."

I hurried up and said loudly, "Good to get our backs to the wind, Ma. That's north, behind us."

Pa strode over, cheroot in one hand. He smiled, taking long puffs. The end flared red, died, and flared again.

"Here, Walter. We can face the winter sun and the stream, and the wind will be to our backs—as Sam said." She sighed. "It will be good to get into a house again, to be all together with a roof over our heads." Jake rolled on his back, kicking his legs out. *He* knew.

"We'll dig into the hill, right, Pa?" Billy asked.

"Mr. Know-It-All William!" I hissed—low enough so Pa wouldn't hear.

"I don't know it all, Sam," he hissed back. "Just what Pa told me."

Pa put a hand on both of our shoulders. "Well, I won't be able to do this without my boys. We've got a lot of work ahead of us."

"Doing what, Pa?" Billy sat and hugged his knees. Jake leaned against him.

Pa swept his arm wide. "First, I'll plow the flat land there—for bricks for the house and a stable for

Ham and Duke. Then we've got to dig out the front of this hill."

I shivered. Like a grave. Couldn't he see that?

Pa squeezed my shoulder. "Earth makes the best kind of house, Sam. Warm in winter and cool in summer, and it doesn't cost us a cent! You'll see, you'll get used to it."

Ma nodded. "We'll all get used to it and come to love it."

"Why, Ma, don't you love it already?" Billy jumped up.

"Not yet, Billy. It's too new, too different. But I will—in time."

Pa sucked in the last smoke from his cheroot and ground it out in the grass. I patted Ma's arm, glad I wasn't the only one who felt that way.

"Well, I love it already, and I know we won't have to take so many baths, right, Ma?" said Billy.

She shook her finger at him. "Every Saturday, same as always, with water from the creek until Pa can dig a well."

I looked out over the flowing grasses running away to the edge of the world. The clouds towered up like giant houses. Birds swooped and called over the prairie. And the wind just blew and blew like nothing got in its way to stop it. Maybe I would get used to it. Maybe.

CHAPTER THIRTEEN

THE NEXT MORNING THE SUN WAS ORANGE ON the horizon. Pa hitched Ham and Duke to the new plow, set the blade into the earth, and started turning over the flat land near the rise. The steam rose white from the horses' noses. The earth rolled out black and pretty. It *smelled* rich. Billy ran over and sniffed it.

"Mmm. Mmm, Sam, this earth is so new and clean, not all used up like Kentucky." He looked up and grinned, but I couldn't answer him. How could he leave everything behind and not mind? How?

Pa waved at us both and handed Billy a spade and me a shovel. "See, boys, this strip of earth the plow turns up will always be twelve inches wide and four inches thick."

He knotted a string and gave it to me. "That's two feet, Sam. You just measure off on this strip of dirt and cut it into a brick every two feet. Billy, you smooth off the edges so they'll fit tight together."

"Yes, Pa."

I held the string against the dark strip of earth and then jabbed at it with my spade. The spade bounced off and I coughed. I tried again, pushing down hard, and the spade sliced through the tangled roots.

"Not easy, is it, Sam?" Billy watched.

"Well, *you* try!"

Billy smoothed the edges with his spade, and I was glad to see they were pretty ragged.

Pa plowed, I cut, and Billy watched a hawk sailing overhead.

"Stop dreaming, we've got work to do."

"We'll always have work to do, Sam. Isn't this sky just something, the way it goes on and on?"

I couldn't tell him how it made the back of my neck feel, all prickly and naked. There was too much sky and too much wind, and I wanted to get into that house so bad my teeth ached.

"Get to work, Billy. I want to get our house built!"

He put his foot to the spade and smoothed the side of a brick. "What's the hurry, Sam? There's nothing to be afraid of."

I had all I could do not to jump on him. What

did he mean by *afraid*? I wasn't afraid, just responsible. I saw Pa looking over from the end of the row, so I gritted my teeth and said, "I'm not afraid. I—just—want—to—get"—I jabbed at the dirt—"into—our—house!"

"Anything you say, Sam." Billy worked faster then, and I wondered how his agreeing with me could sound sassier than just about anything.

ALL AFTERNOON WE JABBED AND SHAPED bricks. I thought of Grandpa's words, "Huh! This is the future?" In my mind, I could see our farmhouse back home, how white and sunny it was.

"These will be our walls," I said after a while.

"Mmm?" Billy straightened and groaned.

I poked at a dark, grassy brick. "Do you think they'll keep the rain out—and the wind?"

"Should do, Sam. Pa seems to think so."

Pa. He walked behind the horses at the far end of the row. I knew he was tired, but he had a spring in his step. These would be *his* bricks, *his* walls. Not Grandpa's.

"Do you think it'll be warm in the winter?" I watched Billy smooth the edges.

"Probably, Sam. I don't know." Suddenly, he looked lost and small under that big sky. "You keep asking me questions, Sam, and I don't know the answers. I'm only ten years old, remember?"

I took the spade from his hand and made him sit down. "You look kind of pale, Billy. I know what Grandpa'd say about this work—'Work for field hands!' That's what *he'd* say."

Billy mopped his brow. "He would say that. Harold did work like this every day for twenty years."

"Harold!"

"He said at the end of the day he couldn't stand up for God or the devil. Let's try lying down, Sam. Harold said that helps."

I didn't like to take Harold's advice, but I tried it, anyway. I was too tired to argue.

"It doesn't help, does it?" Billy chewed on a piece of grass.

"Nope." I sat up and watched Ma walking toward us.

"Walter!" Ma called, at the edge of the plowed field. "Coffee! Come, boys."

Pa kept plowing for a minute, almost like he'd forgotten how to stop. He tore off some grass, rubbed Ham and Duke's sides, and gave them a bucket of water.

Ma set down the blue enameled pot, and we sat on the grass. The coffee steamed in the air. Ma's face looked calm and clear, like the wind had swept away whatever worries she had. She handed Billy a blue cup.

"Coffee, now, William. I guess if you're old

enough to build a house, you're old enough to drink coffee."

Billy grinned, took a sip, and choked. I thumped him. "Maybe"—he set the cup down—"maybe I'll just have water today, Ma."

I poured him a cup from the water jug and smiled. I was glad he didn't like coffee. I drank it and liked it. I had to have *something* that Billy didn't get, that he was too young for. That was only fair.

_____

I COULDN'T SLEEP THAT NIGHT. My back wouldn't let me. Even though Pa stopped work early to let us and the horses rest, it was still a *long* afternoon.

Pa snored softly, and Billy was curled up on his side of the mattress. I crept out the back of the wagon and dropped to the ground.

The moon was out, and the grass was silver. Ham and Duke grazed, swishing their tails and stomping. I whistled. Jake crawled out from under the wagon and followed me.

I wished I had Pa's gun with me, but I just *had* to walk. The prairie flowed away to the end of the sky, and the grass rustled. I went up to the rise where our house would be. The moon made the grass silver. An owl called, "Too-whoo, too-whoo." I stamped my feet. Under this spot we would live, dug into the earth. It still felt like digging a grave, no matter what Pa said.

With Jake at my side, I ran to the edge of the creek bluff. Below, the water was dark with silver bits on top. I wished I were a fish, quiet under some dark bank. They didn't have to worry about houses and heavy earth and wolves and Indians.

Jake whined and nudged my leg. He didn't worry. Nor did Billy. It seemed only me, Samuel T. White, knew about the dangerous things out here.

A howl sounded in the distance, a long, rising note. I ran fast as I could back to the wagon and jumped into bed.

"That you, Sam?"

"Yes." I pulled the covers over my nose.

"Where were you?"

"By the creek."

"Oh." He put his head back down on the pillow. "Was it pretty, Sam?"

"Yes, Billy." Pretty lonely, I wanted to add. Pretty wild.

CHAPTER FOURTEEN

BILLY AND I CARRIED BUCKETS OF DIRT AWAY from the front of the hill Pa was digging out. After a week of cutting bricks, we had enough for the house and barn and now were helping Pa ready the site.

I got the shivers every time I looked at that black, deep hole. "Looks like a grave," I whispered to Billy. Didn't want Pa to hear. He'd think I was complaining, and then I might not get my rifle in the fall. Once we were rich.

"I like it." Billy rested a moment and looked at it. "It'll be like the houses we used to make back home when we were little. Remember?"

I did remember. Grandma'd set out her old quilts

and blankets on a rainy, cold winter's day. Billy and I would put them over chairs and tables to make houses underneath. They were cozy and warm, a place for telling stories.

Suddenly I felt better. "An earth-blanket house, is that it, Billy?"

"That's it, Sam." Billy lifted a bucket of dirt, carried it off to the side, and dumped it.

"One more bucket to go," I sang.

"One more bucket it is," he sang back, leaning to the side under the weight of the bucket. I had to admire him then. He was smaller than me, and he carried the dirt off as good as I did.

Ham and Duke blew through their noses, "Whoosh!" as Pa drove the wagon up. We climbed in, Billy and I, and loaded bricks all that afternoon to be ready the next morning. It took both of us to lift one sod brick, though Pa could heft one all by himself.

Ma walked over from the wagon, where she'd been cleaning all of our clothes and stuff for the house.

"Can't I help, Walt? I could lift, or watch the horses. Something!"

"No, Ellie." Pa set a brick in the wagon. "This work's too heavy for a woman. Besides, I promised the colonel that I wouldn't let you get all shriveled up like Millie—"

"Millie!" Ma interrupted. "You need help, Walt."

Pa just said, "Tchaa." Ma sighed and went back to the wagon.

———

IT WAS GRAY AND WINDY WHEN PA SET UP A line from two cottonwood poles to keep the bricks straight for the front wall. I couldn't see how a line that blew in the breeze would become a wall—something that would keep out wind, wolves, and snow.

"Okay, boys." Pa jumped down from the wagon. "Sam, you and Billy hand me the sod bricks from the wagon, and I'll stack them up for the front wall."

All morning he stacked up the bricks beneath the line, leaving an open space for the front door. The wall got higher and higher. After lunch, Pa smoothed down some cottonwood poles with his ax and notched them into a frame for the door—two on one side and one on top for the lintel. He made a square frame for the front window, hammered it together, and set that on top of the bricks.

By the time dusk came, we'd finished the front and one small side wall. Pa'd fixed it so the hill met the left edge of the house front, but we had to build a piece of the right-hand wall to fit into the hill.

"There." Pa took his shovel and packed dirt firmly around the bricks. Where they met the slope they made a nice, snug fit. Ma joined him, shoveling dirt beside him, and tamping it into the cracks with a stick.

"Now, Ellie, I promised the colonel—" Pa began.

"Hush!" Ma said. "He's in Kentucky, we're here, and you need another pair of hands."

Pa rubbed his mustache.

Ma looked at him, and I could feel the air between them, like the green sky before a thunderstorm. Then Pa lifted his shoulders and let them drop. "All right, Ellie. I don't like it, but I do admit we can use the help."

We finished tamping dirt in the cracks and stood back. Pa took off his hat and lit a cheroot. "Look at that, will you?"

Billy bowed to the house. "Our first wall."

Our first wall, I said to myself. We'd done it. No one else had helped. No one told us what to do or blew bugles. I patted the wall. It was thick and solid, with tufts of grass in the cracks. Something fierce and spicy rose in me. The same feeling I had when I tasted Pa's corn liquor—before I got sick, that is.

———

THE NEXT DAY MA RUBBED GOOSE GREASE INTO Pa's shoulders. She didn't even ask if she could help but just took her place beside Billy and me as Pa set a large, forked log by the front wall. He put another one opposite it against the north wall, then fitted a ridge pole in the forks. I handed him cottonwood poles, which he nailed against the ridge pole and down against poles laid on top of the east and west walls.

Billy and I cut willow brush from the creek bed; Ma helped load it in the wagon. When we brought it back to the dugout, Pa showed the three of us how to weave it over and under the poles, making a kind of netting between the rafters. Then he laid straw on top and put more sod bricks down carefully for the roof.

"Come, boys." He motioned to us. "Bring some dirt up in those buckets, and we'll tamp it down good." We shoveled dirt on top of the sod that had its grass side up and tamped it down in any cracks we could see.

"Ma's feet are perfect for this," Billy said as she tramped over the roof. Billy was better at tamping than carrying, and I started to complain, but Pa just looked hard at me, and I said nothing. When we were done, Ma crouched and patted the earth.

"I declare, Walter, it's a roof, a real roof."

Pa was too tired to smile, but he did squeeze her hand. "A roof for my Ellie."

She patted the roof again and gave Billy and me a proud smile. "That's my good boys, helping Pa with all the work. My boys are growing up now." She looked a little sad.

"And it's a good thing!" Pa sat back on his heels

and groaned. "I couldn't have done this without them—or without you." He squeezed Ma's hand, then drew us all to him and hugged us tight. I could feel how much he loved us then, squeezing us together like a big bear hugging its cubs. "Our house, our very own house!" Pa said gruffly.

We climbed down and went through the front door. I made my feet step inside, and I kept looking up at the roof, afraid it might crush us. I knew how much weight was up there. Ma grabbed a broom and began to sweep the floor clean while Billy and I took the extra dirt out in buckets. I began to breathe easier; nothing had fallen in yet, and it was beginning to look like a house.

Once the dirt was cleared away, Pa stood in the doorway. "I want my family close," he said, pulling us tight.

We could see the creek bed and the black trees beside it. The prairie rolled away, green and gold like a carpet. The sun blazed down from a sky so blue it felt heavy.

I shivered, and Pa hugged me tighter. "Cold, son?"

"No, Pa." I didn't know why I shivered. Maybe I was just tired to death. Maybe it was the heavy earth overhead. Or the prairie, so clean and wide and empty.

CHAPTER FIFTEEN

THE SUN WENT DOWN, AND THE SKY STAYED pink and violet for a long time. Through the window opening I saw birds flying across the sunset and wondered where their homes were. Pa came over with some greased paper and began to nail it to the window frame.

"Oh, Pa! I wish you didn't have to."

Ma stopped sweeping and sighed. "Seems like I'm being shut in, Walter. It's contrary of me. I thought I wanted to be under a roof more than anything, but closing up that window . . . "

Pa said, "I'll get glass soon as I can afford it, Ellen."

—

She looked through the window and touched it softly. "It's just that it smudges the outside."

"It won't be for long." Pa nailed the paper tight.

He made a cottonwood frame for their bed against the north wall, next to the hill. Over the mattress Ma spread the red and gold dove quilt that Grandma made, and we all sat on it. It made the room look homey to have something of Grandma's in it.

"We'll put Sam and Billy's bed here, against the west side." Pa hammered some cottonwood poles together and laid the mattress on top.

"I get next to the wall," I whispered, as Pa went outside.

Billy looked at me. "I don't care, Sam."

I hated how he gave in so easy. He knelt and put his clothes underneath the bed, wrapped up in canvas.

"Jake can sleep under the bed, can't he, Ma?" Billy whistled to Jake and patted the earth under the bed.

"I suppose so, William. I certainly don't want him outside at night with—with all there is out there." She shut her lips on the words. Did she worry about wolves, as well as Indians? And did she look at the prairie rolling away so wide and empty that it made your neck prickle up? I didn't dare ask. But I did wonder.

Ma hung a calico curtain across the front of their bed and sang to herself.

The next time Ma and Pa went out to the wagon, I took my knife and carved a tiny niche by my side of the bed.

"Sam!"

"Hush! What they don't know can't hurt them." I reached into the canvas sack that held my things and took out the fossil stone Jeb gave me and the special fish hook from Luke. I set them in the niche and felt better. It was like a tiny room all to myself. It made me feel safe.

Pa staggered in from the wagon, carrying Ma's chest. "This will be our table until we move into a bigger house." He put it under the window, right near the head of our bed. Our house sure was getting crowded.

"All right," Ma said. "Tomorrow, I'm going to make flour paste and put up those newspapers we've been saving on the walls. We need to cover that dirt!"

Pa started a small fire in the cookstove—that was against the right-hand wall—and Ma fried up some salt fish and corn cakes. The smell was sweet in that house, a people smell inside our dirt room.

We sat down. Pa bowed his head and said grace—a nice short one, not all winding like Grandpa's. "Thank you, Lord, for seeing us safely here. Keep us safe and mindful of our blessings. Amen." We all said, "Amen." Jake curled up with a sigh by the table, his head against my foot.

It was our first dinner in our first house with no Grandma, no Grandpa, no Harold nearby. It was just us and the wind and a moon that made a white blur through the window.

When Billy and I climbed into bed, I pulled the covers up tight and sighed. I heard Ma laugh behind the curtain and then Pa snoring.

"Listen," I whispered to Billy.

"To what? Pa's snores?"

"Just listen."

"I can't hear anything," he said after a long time.

"That's just it. I can't hear anything, either." For the first time, I couldn't hear the wind. I smiled and went to sleep.

CHAPTER SIXTEEN

BILLY AND I HITCHED THE HORSES TO THE PLOW the next day and rode out on their backs to the planting field. Pa set the blade down, clucked to the horses, and told us to jump off.

"They've got enough work to do without you two rascals riding them. Go to the stream and peel yourselves some hickory sticks. Sharpen them with the hatchet, Sam, and both of you bring out the sack of seed corn."

"Seed corn, Pa?" I stopped in my tracks. "I thought we were planting wheat this summer. Isn't it wheat that's going to make us rich?"

Pa called over his shoulder as the horses moved away from us. "It will, Sam, it will. All in good time. This ground is too raw for wheat. You can see how the roots tangle up the earth. They'll rot this summer and fall, and next spring we'll harrow the ground fine enough for wheat."

My stomach sank. How could we get rich on sod corn? I bet we wouldn't even make enough money to buy that rifle in the fall.

Billy poked my side. "Stop worrying, Sam. You worry too much. Pa knows what he's doing."

I wanted to say, Somebody's got to do the worrying around here! But I didn't want to get in a fight with Billy. It was too pretty a day.

We found some hickory sticks, peeled them, and brought them to a sharp point with the hatchet. Together we hauled the sack of seed corn out to the field, though by the time we got there, my arms felt like they'd fall off. Billy didn't say a word, but just got redder and redder as we pulled the sack to the edge of the field.

"Thanks, boys!" Pa called as the horses marched toward us. I could smell that sweet earth, and some swallows dipped overhead. Billy and I tied towels around our waists and put handfuls of seed in the folds. Then we punched holes in the sod and dropped the kernels in, tamping them down tight. I could see Ma over by the dugout, working in the garden patch Pa had plowed for her.

"Can we get rich on sod corn?" I whispered to Billy.

He dropped some corn into the dark hole. "Don't know, Sam. Maybe it's next year we'll get rich."

Ahead of us, Pa turned and smiled. "Don't worry, boys, I can still sell sod corn in town. It won't bring as much as wheat, but it'll help us get by till next year. *Then* you'll see something. This land is just *made* for wheat!"

But I did worry. I wanted that rifle—to protect myself, to go hunting with. And it looked like that rifle was a long way off.

━━━━━━━━━━━━━

IT TOOK US A WEEK TO PLANT THAT FIELD, AND what with building the barn for Ham and Duke, the corn was already up and green when Pa said, "Take the day off, boys. You've both been working ever since we got here. Go fishing. Go exploring."

Billy looked at me and grinned. We grabbed our fishing poles and set off for the creek. Jake bounded beside us. The grass was full of little flowers—purple, blue, and yellow. Clouds raced overhead, the shadows skittering over us. Billy kept taking deep breaths.

"This air!" he swung his arms. "I could eat it, Sam, it's so good."

I fiddled with my pole. "Don't you miss home, Billy? I liked Kentucky air—nice and warm."

"Too warm!" Billy picked some flowers and stuck them in his pocket. "For Ma."

It annoyed me how that boy was always thinking up things to please Ma.

"Well, *I* liked Kentucky." I slid down the creek bank.

" 'Course you did, Sam." Billy landed with a thump by the stream. "You liked living with Grandpa and all those rules."

I turned quick. "What's *that* supposed to mean?"

"Why, nothing, Sam." Billy stroked Jake's head. "Just that you liked rules and all, and Grandpa's bugle, and I didn't."

"That's 'cause you're no soldier." I stabbed a worm with my hook.

"Don't want to be a soldier." Billy let his line float in the water. "Didn't look to me like it got anyone anywhere. Pa got wounded—still hurts his shoulder, you know that. The war just made Grandpa grumpy, as far as I can see, and it took his land away. Only good thing was Harold got to be free."

I spat into the water. My chest felt hot and tight. "Harold! What will he do with his freedom? I ask you? Much good it did him. The war was important, Billy. You're just too young to understand." I breathed quickly and watched my line. If he caught a fish before me, I'd be *really* mad.

Billy scratched his head. "I don't know, Sam. I know soldiers think wars are important, but I don't think anything's worth dying for. Would you die for our sod house?"

I sucked in a breath. For Ma and Pa? To protect Grandma and her peach pies on the windowsill? "Sure I would. Just like Grandpa went to war. Sure."

Then I missed Grandpa so much my throat choked up. I missed that bugle. I missed Grandma and her tiny eyeglasses and her apron that smelled like apples. I missed the linden tree and the cool shade under it in summer. I missed Luke calling to me to go fishing, and Jeb and his jokes. I thought that when we got our house built I wouldn't miss Kentucky anymore, that it would make it all right. But it didn't. I guess that home isn't a house. It's something else. I didn't know how I was going to get it, and that made me so sad I wanted to hit Billy for looking so comfortable and easy by that strange, northern stream.

CHAPTER SEVENTEEN

Billy just sat there, fishing. Sometimes he'd flick his blond hair back; sometimes he'd reach out and scratch Jake's head. It wasn't fair!

I set my fishing pole over my shoulder and strode upstream.

"Sam!" Billy called. "Wait for me!"

"Don't come," I called over my shoulder. "I want to go someplace on my own—just once. On my own!" Jake whined, followed me for a bit, then ran back to Billy and licked his hand. I kept walking farther and farther upstream, and finally Jake howled. I could hear Billy saying something to him, then I turned a corner and they were gone.

The wind blew. A bird sang in a willow. I kicked at a rock and slowed down. What were Jeb and Luke doing now? Fishing? Maybe they were lying on their backs and telling jokes. Or Jeb could be feeding the catfish in a pool of his. Sometimes he'd bring corn bread from home and get the fish used to coming to a special pool for food. He'd set in his line and hook and just wait to pull out those fat fish. I walked and walked until my feet got tired and my shoulder ached from the bouncing fishing pole.

Something barked sharply once, twice, off to my left. I wheeled around. Sometimes Indians made sounds like foxes to warn others. Maybe I was near a village and didn't even know it. I stopped, listened, crept up the bank, and looked over the top.

Grass waving in the wind. Clouds galloping overhead. I wished I had Jake with me. I couldn't see any tepees or men on horses. But smoke smudged the sky, and something white caught my eye. I ducked down. It could be a tepee with a cooking fire.

I peeked over the bank. Sun glinted on something in a low hill. Glass! It was a window. Indians didn't have glass, so it had to be a house. I jumped up and ran toward it. When I got closer, I saw the dugout door set into the hill and the window shining in the sun. A lady in a striped dress was sweeping out the door and singing. A baby in a bonnet sat out front. Behind the dugout a girl was hanging wash on a clothesline, and farther back a man and a boy were hoeing weeds in a cornfield.

"Ho!" I shouted, and ran forward. The woman stuck her broom in front, like a rifle, grabbed the baby, and ran inside.

"Hello! I'm a friend. From downstream. White's my name. Samuel T. White. Hey, don't be scared."

The woman poked her head out of the dugout, still holding her baby tight. She walked slowly toward me, then smiled and ran forward.

"Sam, Sam White, I do declare. Whatever are *you* doing here? Are your folks with you? Did you say you lived downstream? Why, Peter will never believe this. What luck! Allan will be glad to see you. Just yesterday he was complaining about only having girls to talk to, and didn't he just wish he had a friend nearby." She stopped and took a breath. "And, oh, my, won't I be glad to see another woman again." She buried her face in her baby's bonnet.

"Mrs. Grant. But you were going west—to the coast, last time we saw you. Did you say Allan was wishing—?"

"Oh, we were," she interrupted. "But everyone got to fighting—the men, the boys, even the women. It was as nasty as a hornet's nest, and Mr. Grant always says he won't stand for bad feeling among friends, so"—she straightened the baby's bonnet— "here we are."

The girl, who I remembered was Amanda, came up and stood shyly by Mrs. Grant. She asked, "How's your brother, Billy?"

I said, "The same as ever." Then Allan ran up and clapped me on the shoulder. "Pa and me saw you from the field. 'Visitors!' Pa yelled, and off we went. Isn't this the strangest thing! Sam White, our neighbor."

I just smiled at him. Words are hard when you're happy all of a sudden. I clapped him on the shoulder, and he touched my fishing pole.

"Isn't that creek just full of fish? Pa and I've been fishing most every day since we got here."

Mr. Grant held out his hand. "My, we're glad to see you, Sam White. I look forward to seeing your pa and ma. And your brother, Billy?"

I nodded, not able to get a word in.

"Guess he must have found you all right that time. You're the first neighbors we've seen since we got here. There's some others to the west of us, but haven't met them yet, and we've been too busy to go into town. Seems like my mouth is getting rusty."

"Why don't you boys go off—Allan, you can leave your work for now," Mr. Grant said. "Then come back and have something to drink in the dugout before you go home, Sam."

Allan and I went to the creek, sliding down the bank. We sat on some rocks. Allan pointed to a deep pool. "Put your line in that, Sam. That's full of fat ones."

I peered into the pool. In the dark water, I saw a fin waving. Sun gleamed purple and pink. "Trout!"

Allan nodded. Wouldn't Jeb just like this, I thought to myself.

I dug up a beetle, baited my hook, and let it float on the creek.

Allan hugged his legs to his chest. "Well, I tell you, this is good luck. I'm awful sick of talking to Amanda, and baby Ben doesn't say much yet."

"Babies don't, do they?"

Allan laughed and threw a stone downstream. A kingfisher rattled by. "I saw a mink here yesterday. Pa and me are thinking of setting a trap line when it gets cold."

"Me, too. Then we could sell our furs in town and buy things."

"Get me a rifle," Allan said. "You never know when you're going to need one."

"No, sir. You surely don't know when you'll need a rifle."

Neither of us said that word, *Indians*, but I knew he was thinking it same as me. I felt naked on the prairie without a rifle, even though the fort was thirty miles away.

"Do you think—" He stopped.

"Don't worry about scaring the fish. I don't care

about *them*. I can fish any old time. Can't always talk."

He rubbed his nose. "Anyone talking about school yet, Sam? My ma does go on about it."

"Not yet." Something snapped at the beetle, and the line floated free. "I hoped we couldn't go—being too far from town and all."

"Ha! They'll get a school up, just you watch. Might be at someone's house. My ma might want your ma to get up a small school, if she's got books."

"Oh, she's got books, all right." I sighed and yanked my line out of the water. "My brother, Billy, would like that. Not me!"

"Me, neither." Allan threw a stone into the air.

Suddenly, I didn't mind. "Well, if there *is* going to be a school, we'll be there together. We can meet every day."

He grinned. "That's true. There's always recess, and if it's faraway, we can ride our horses to school. You still got your dog, Jake?"

I nodded.

"Bring him, too. School won't be so bad with a dog, eh, Sam?"

I slung my pole over my shoulder. The sun was getting low in the sky, and Ma would worry if I didn't get home soon. "Let's get that drink your ma promised."

We went back to the dugout where Mrs. Grant showed me how she'd fixed it all up, with newspaper on the walls and little bits of things on shelves. She gave us cool mint tea in tin cups. It tasted good and fresh.

"I can't wait to see your ma." Mrs. Grant sighed and clasped her hands. "To see another woman out in the middle of these prairies . . ." She set the tin cup down with a bang. Mr. Grant looked over and away, quick.

"They are awful big, aren't they?" I said.

She smiled. "Yes, Sam, they are awful big, and the wind blows all the time, and I miss my friends."

"So do I."

I think she almost kissed me then, but instead, got up and wrapped a loaf of new bread in a napkin. "You take this back to your ma and tell her to come visit just as soon as she can."

"And tell your pa that we can share work if he needs help," Mr. Grant said.

"Yes, sir." I waved to them in the dugout door, and Allan came with me to the bluff overlooking the creek. He clapped me on the shoulder again, and I said, "I think I'm going to like Dakota Territory."

CHAPTER EIGHTEEN

"Mrs. Grant, did you say? Two miles down-stream?" Ma jumped up from the table.

"Now, Ellie." Pa took her hand. "You can't go see her tonight. It's getting dark. Tomorrow we'll all go over for a visit."

"Remember Amanda?" Billy crunched on the new lettuce from Ma's garden. "I did like that girl. I was teaching her how to blow grass flutes, you know, the way Grandpa taught us."

"And I can talk with Pete." Pa laid down his fork and wiped the vinegar from his mustache. "We can share work if we need to. Did you say they'd got their house and barn all built, Sam?"

"Yes, Pa. Everything's all done. They were

hoeing corn when I found them."

"It's Providence." Ma sat down with a sigh. "You can't tell me it's an accident they're living just downstream from us. We all needed friends and here they are." She smiled at us.

"Don't forget the ones we left behind," I whispered.

"I haven't forgot, Sam," Billy whispered back. "I remember Harold."

I don't think Pa and Ma heard us, they were so busy clanking dishes and talking about the visit they'd make next day. But I smiled at Billy then; maybe he wasn't so comfy up here, up North. Even if it was an ex-slave he missed, at least he missed *somebody!*

———

THE NEXT DAY PA TOOK US OUT TO THE CORNfield. He rocked on his heels and smiled. The green leaves were up to Pa's knees now, and the field was thick and dark with corn.

"Looks like a good crop, Pa," I said. "We should get some money for that." And we had helped to do it, Billy and me.

"We should, Sam. This earth is just made for crops. Why, I think if I left my plow out here, it'd grow a new one overnight."

Ma patted his arm. "We were right to come, Walter. This is a land of promise."

What kind of promise? I wanted to ask, but didn't. If I wanted to get that rifle this fall after the corn was harvested, I'd better not ask any hard questions or be too sassy.

"Do you know what day this is, Sam?" Pa smiled.

"No, Pa." All the days seemed pretty much the same to me.

"It's the Fourth of July." He squeezed Ma's waist. "Independence Day for all of us. By gosh, I like being on my own!"

"Fourth of July!" Billy's face fell. "There's no one to make speeches, Pa! And no firecrackers."

"We'll just have to make our own celebration, Billy," Pa said.

Ma led us back to the dugout. "Sam, you wrap the last of that smoked ham from home. William, get some new lettuce from the garden, and I'll make lemonade. Well, vinegar ade is what I'll make."

Soon, we were packed and ready. Pa and Billy hitched up Ham and Duke, while I lifted the heavy picnic basket into the wagon.

Pa flicked the reins, and we set off across the rolling grass. Jake trotted beside the wagon, ears pricked. Pa whistled, and Billy and I lay on blankets in the back, watching hawks overhead.

When we saw the smoke from the Grants' dugout, Ma stood in the wagon and shaded her eyes. "Why, it's just like our place, Walter. Look at that!" We could see their cornfield in back, thick and green like ours.

The Grants ran across the grass rise, waving their arms and shouting. "Hello, hello, welcome!"

"Happy Fourth of July!" Pa stood up and shouted. "Independence Day, neighbors!"

I've seen spring cows look like that when let out of a barn. They race around a field, kicking up their heels and touching each other's noses. Billy chased Amanda across the grass. Pa started talking crops with Mr. Grant while Ma chatted with Mrs. Grant. The baby just looked and looked, his eyes so big they almost fell out of his face.

"Let's go get some prairie dogs, Sam." Allan waved his slingshot. "There's a hill of them about a mile west of here."

"Don't be too long, boys," Pa called. "We'll be eating lunch soon."

I told Billy to keep hold of Jake, and we ran through the grass, so tall now it rubbed my elbows as I ran. It smelled thick and warm like new bread. The cloud shadows smoked across the land ahead of us, and a hot wind blew.

Allan ran faster and faster, and I raced to keep up with him. We stayed neck and neck, neither of us pulling ahead. And once I looked just to make sure. He wasn't any taller than I was!

"Here we are!" Allan dropped to the grass, panting. I couldn't tell we were anyplace different.

"There," he pointed. I peered over the grass and saw a big mound not far from us. It was all pockmarked with holes, and little brown animals scurried back and forth, just like people visiting in a busy town. A few of them seemed posted like guards at the edges of the mound. They stood on their hind feet and looked in our direction. We stayed quiet in the grass for a long time. Then they barked, but it didn't sound like a warning.

When I looked again, they were still busy as ever. I guess they hadn't seen us—yet.

Allan took out his slingshot and put a round rock in it. "I'm going to sneak up around the north side, downwind, and see if I can get one. Coming?"

I hesitated a moment, then followed him, crawling through the grass. I didn't like it. Didn't like the idea of killing one of those little brown, striped animals. Fish are one thing. And raccoons are just a nuisance. These were different, more like people.

We crept downwind of them, and I could hear the sound of them living together in that mound—a busy, scuffling sound. Feet hurrying back and forth, little barks and grunts and sounds that maybe a mother made to her pups.

Allan raised himself slowly and pulled back his slingshot. I had all I could do not to yell, "Stop!"

A hawk did it for me. Swooping high overhead, it dove over the mound. The prairie dogs barked, and suddenly, the mound was empty.

I smiled.

"Darn!" Allan stood. "That's done it. They won't be out for a while. They are the cagiest critters you ever saw. I've been here half a dozen times, and I haven't got one yet." He swung his slingshot and began to run. "Race you home to lunch!"

I ran beside him, pumping my arms, faster and faster. I thought of that hawk in the high windy sky, how his wings would carry him. I thought of my arms as wings and my feet as claws, grabbing the ground. I edged past Allan, faster, then farther out in front until we burst through the high grass to the dugout.

"Beat you!" I gasped, and landed with a thump on the picnic blanket beside Billy.

Allan lay beside me, grinning. I liked that in a friend, that he didn't mind if he lost in a fair race. Some people get all testy and cranky.

"Here, Sam." Mrs. Grant handed me a plate of smoked ham, new lettuce, beans, corn relish, and bread. We all kept pretty busy for a while, just eating. Even Billy forgot to talk and ate. Amanda wiped her fingers like a dainty little girl, but I saw how she wolfed the food down, same as us. Mrs. Grant and Ma talked about recipes for relish, putting in their gardens, and trying to keep a dugout clean. Pa and Mr. Grant talked about horses being better than oxen. We kept quiet, the way kids are supposed to when grown-ups are talking.

Mr. Grant set down his coffee cup and smiled. "My, that's about all I can eat. I don't know if I'm fuller from seeing folks or from eating."

"I think people are as good as food any day," Billy said.

"They certainly are." Mrs. Grant patted his arm. "You do know a lot for such a young boy."

What was it that made women like him so? I'd never figure it out. I could tell Allan thought the same as he rolled his eyes at me.

"I've got a surprise for us," Mr. Grant said.

"A speech?" Billy looked up from the grass flute he was making for Amanda. "About freedom and the future?"

"No, I'm no good at speeches, son." Mr. Grant went back to the dugout. He came out, waving something in his hand. "A Roman candle. I brought one all the way from Tennessee."

Ma said, "But we can't wait until dark, Mr. Grant. We've got to get back before then." She didn't say the word, but we all knew it was better to be home before dark.

"I know that, Mrs. White," he said. "We'll do it now."

"Wait until a cloud comes over the sun." Billy sat down beside me. "Then we'll see it better."

Mr. Grant set out a pitcher of water for us to douse the grass where the firecracker would land. We sat and watched the sky, the clouds blowing by like giant, gray wash on a line. Jake nosed my hand, and I patted his warm head.

"There's a few gathering," Mr. Grant pointed. "You could light it soon, Walter."

Mr. Grant set the Roman candle in a spot away from the blanket. Allan and I tore away all the grass nearby, and Pa brought over his matches and case.

The clouds came closer, closer, a wind came up, and Pa said, "Now!" He struck the match. It flared, and he held it to the firecracker string. It sputtered up the line, stopped, then raced to the candle bottom.

Foom! It shot up the sky, across those dark, gray clouds, like a falling star going the wrong way.

"Oh, my!" Mrs. Grant said. Ham snorted and shied, kicking his heels, and Jake raced around, barking.

Allan and I watched to see where it would fall and ran, carrying the water pitcher. The firecracker sputtered out and dropped into the grass. We found it, still smoking a little. Allan poured water on the spot and picked up the candle in a gunnysack. We brought it back.

Pa sighed. "Well, I don't know about you folks,

but this is the best Fourth of July celebration I've ever had in Dakota Territory."

Mr. Grant lay back on the blanket and roared. I didn't know people could laugh with their mouths upside down—big belly laughs.

When I closed my eyes, I could see that firecracker flaming up the sky. And when I opened them, I saw everyone gathered on the blanket, smiling and talking in soft voices. I felt at home, for the first time.

CHAPTER NINETEEN

Each night when I went to bed, I touched the little niche in the wall. There was the fish hook from Luke; there was the fossil stone from Jeb.

Billy nudged me. "Slave superstition!"

"Isn't!" I hissed. "Didn't they see us safe across the Mississippi?"

"Yes." Billy sighed. We didn't say the colt's name, but I knew he remembered—just like me. And each time I touched my good-luck things, I thanked them for sending me a friend, and thanked them that the corn grew so thick and tall.

We took so many fish out of the creek that Pa said he was going to grow fins. But he grinned when he said it and always reminded me, "It means we don't have to buy from the store, Sam. You're helping us settle this land."

That just made us go back for more, and Mrs. Grant and Ma kept sharing ideas about how to cook up those fish. On a hot day at the beginning of August, she sat beside Ma in the shade, snapping beans from the garden.

"I roll them in cornmeal and fry them," Ma said.

"Mmmm, or rolled in flour with some greens underneath." Mrs. Grant smiled and fanned baby Ben. That was the solemnest baby I ever did see. He never smiled, just looked at you and looked like he was eating up the world with his eyes.

Billy and I sat in the shade, brushing flies away. "It's hot as Hades," Billy said, slumping over on his side.

"William!" Ma reproved.

"Well, it is hot as Hades. That isn't a swear, Ma, it's in the Bible. Isn't it, Sam?" he whispered.

"Maybe so, William, but it's as near a swear as you can get and I don't want to hear it again!"

Billy made a face at me. "Want to go fishing?"

"Nope. Too hot. Too many flies." Down by the creek it would be cooler, but the bugs'd be worse.

Billy flicked at the flies with one hand. "Poor horses," he sighed. We watched Pa tethering Ham and Duke in the shade of the sod barn. Their tails swished back and forth. They stamped, and Ham's big sides shuddered to keep the flies off.

Pa came and flopped down beside us. "It's too hot to work today. Hope it won't hurt the corn," he worried.

"Now, Walter, the corn can survive a little heat. As long as we keep getting some rain."

"Haven't had much of *that*!" Pa said.

None of us said any more. It felt like bad luck to talk too much about the corn crop and what might go wrong. It was like looking backward over your shoulder when you went past a graveyard; as long as you *didn't* look, no ghosts could get you.

"Everything'll be just fine," Mrs. Grant said. I wanted to hush her, not to say more, but she went on. "We'll harvest the crops and get a good price, Pete says. Then we'll all be riding in buggies and dressing in silks, isn't that so, Ellie?"

"I hope so, Mary." She pushed at her wet hair and fanned baby Ben. He lay on the grass, looking up at the sky and played with his toes.

Allan and I had it all worked out. Once the crops were sold, we were both going to get rifles and go hunting together—maybe for coyotes. With what we could shoot and trap come winter, we'd have money of our own next spring.

Then the baby began to cry, a high, fretful sound.

Mrs. Grant picked him up and joggled him back and forth.

"Here." Ma handed her a wet cloth, and Mrs. Grant patted Ben's face. He just cried harder.

Then the horses began to stamp and shy. First Ham—the nervous one—then Duke. Pa pointed to the sky. It was dark and smoky.

"Must be a storm coming. Quick, boys, help with the horses." We ran to the barn and Pa got Ham inside while Billy and I untethered Duke and put him in the barn. Once inside, they calmed down a bit, but Ham still tossed his head and rolled his eyes.

"They're spooked," Pa said, wiping his brow. "Don't know why, but something's got into them. I don't like the look of that sky. Maybe there's a thunderstorm coming."

We went back to the dugout, and Ma gave us water in a tin cup. The baby still cried.

"Shhh, let me have Ben," Billy said. Mrs. Grant hesitated, then handed him over. Billy snuggled the baby against his shoulder and walked up to the top of the dugout. "Maybe there's a breeze up here," he called down. The baby's head bobbed against his shoulder, and the crying stopped.

Billy watched the sky, and I watched him. He looked nervous, too, like the horses. The sun dimmed as the clouds came up. Suddenly, Billy cricked his neck back and shouted. He ran downhill to us, holding tight to the baby.

"There's something in those clouds, Pa, can't you see?" He pointed.

The clouds rolled toward us, like a big wind pushed them. The light was a strange, hard gray. At first they looked like everyday clouds, but then I began to see things in them.

"There's something moving in them!" Mrs. Grant yelled. "Small things."

"Insects!" Pa said in an awful voice. "Locusts!" They began to fall from the sky. Brown things falling, *plunk!* on Ma's bonnet. *Plunk!* on the baby's head and on Mrs. Grant's striped dress. *Thunk!* they landed on the garden.

We just stood there a moment, frozen, then Ma shouted, "My garden!" She ran into the dugout and came back with gunnysacks. Mrs. Grant took her baby from Billy, rushed him into the dugout, tied him to the bedpost, and shut the door. They ran to the garden and ripped out the rows of lettuce and tiny, new carrots. The grasshoppers rained down on us, and it was hard to see. Ma and Mrs. Grant looked like people working in clouds of smoke.

Pa shouted, "My rifle! Boys, you grab shovels, anything you can find from the barn and get out to the cornfield!"

Billy and I ran to the barn and grabbed rakes and shovels and raced out to the cornfield. Pa ran around the edge, shooting his rifle.

Capow! A small cloud lifted, then settled. He threw his hat on the ground and set off another volley. *Capow! Capow! Capow!*

I hit at them with the shovel, but for every ten I squished, another twenty fell from the sky. Brown bodies hanging on green leaves. Brown jaws tearing into the unripe corn. Billy struck at them with the spade, but nothing made any difference. All the time we raced around, trying to scare them off, no one said a word. Their crunching filled our ears.

Pa fired until all his bullets were gone. Then he shouted, "Sam, we'll dig a trench as far as we can in the plowed edge of the field. Billy, grab all the grass and twigs you can find. Pile them in the trench."

Pa and I dug as fast as we could in the hard ground. The dirt flew to the side, and the grasshoppers fell on my hat, chewed on my collar. Their raspy claws poked through my shirt, but I couldn't stop digging.

Billy ran up with arms full of grass and threw it into the trench. Pa pulled out his matches and lit the grass. It flared and caught, sending smoke up in dark clouds. The grasshoppers seemed to rise over the smoke for a moment. Pa put his hat on and cheered.

Then the grasshoppers fell into the trench, *plunk!* They fell on top of each other, again and again. The fire sputtered and died. Pa just looked at it. He turned but did not see us.

"It's no use. Nothing will scare them. There's too many." He picked up his hat, wiped the grasshoppers off, and jammed it on his head. "Come back to the dugout, boys."

He turned, and we followed, Billy dragging the shovel behind. His face looked green, and his jaws were clamped tight. I clamped mine, too, afraid that I'd eat one of them if I breathed through my mouth. I felt sick and greasy inside, with those little claws clutching at my shirt and back and their bodies squishing under my feet. They were so deep now, it was like walking through a pile of leaves—brown, moving leaves.

Mrs. Grant and Ma were still outside, flapping at the garden with those sacks. Pa yelled, "Come inside! It's no good, Ellen."

I went to help carry in the sacks of vegetables they'd picked, when Mrs. Grant began to scream.

"Ellen! Ellen! They're eating my dress. Get them off me!"

All along the green stripes of her dress, the grasshoppers were chewing. Pieces of white cloth fell to the ground. Pa ran into the dugout, and brought out

Grandma's quilt. He wrapped it tight around her and pulled it off, taking most of the grasshoppers with it. She yelled, with loud, rising screams, and Pa hurried her inside. I slammed the door shut behind us. We brushed the grasshoppers off each other and stamped them dead.

"Ooooh, ooooh, get them off me!" Mrs. Grant beat at her tattered dress. "Get them off me!"

"They're off, Mary, it's all right," Ma soothed her, brushing the last grasshoppers from her and squishing them with a shovel.

"Shhh, shhh," Pa said between her loud screams. He ran to Grandma's trunk and took out a small brown bottle. "Here, drink this!" He tipped it to her lips, and she sputtered and choked.

"More!" He tipped it again. She swallowed, coughed, sobbed a little, and was quiet. Blessedly quiet. The baby sat on the floor by the bed, whimpering, his eyes wide and scared.

Billy went over and untied Ben, holding him tight against his chest. His eyes, over Ben's shoulder, looked just as wide and scared. Pa stood in the middle of the room as wet as if he'd been in a rainstorm. Ma dabbed at her face with a handkerchief and kept repeating, "My heavens. Who would've ever thought. Who!" She shook herself, patted Mrs. Grant's hand, and drew out the water pail from under the table.

She skimmed grasshoppers from it and filled a tin cup.

"Here. Drink this, Mary." Mrs. Grant hiccupped and drank.

"Ooooh, ooooh," she kept sighing. "Ooooh, their little feet." Ma drank some water, then Pa, and Billy, and I swallowed it down. Just to make the taste of them go away.

Bits of white clung to the seams around Mrs. Grant's shoulders and waist, along with a few ragged pieces of green. Her pantaloons and underwear showed through. I flushed and Ma took Mrs. Grant's arm.

"Come with me," she said, leading Mrs. Grant to their corner of the house. Ma drew the curtain and dressed her in a workday dress—the yellow one with brown spots on it.

"They won't eat brown!" Ma said grimly as she led Mrs. Grant to a chair. "I'm sorry about your dress, Mary. That was your favorite."

Mrs. Grant tried to laugh, but all that came out was a little squeak.

Billy looked at me, and his eyes were hollow. Pa stood by the table, peering out the paper window. He didn't say one word. He didn't even sigh. Just kept his shoulders rigid and hard as a soldier in battle.

Ma sat suddenly in a chair. "My, I feel all used

up." Her voice was shaky. She opened the gunny-sacks and took out the vegetables. "Billy and Sam, you brush off these—these things—and put the vegetables in the washpan."

"Oh, my, what about Pete, what about Pete." Mrs. Grant rocked back and forth. "All alone back home with no one to help him but Amanda and Allan. Poor Pete." She blew her nose, and I could see she was trying hard not to cry. Suddenly, she buried her face in her arms and began to sob. "We have nothing, Ellen, nothing at all. We borrowed to buy the seed. Don't you see what this means?" She turned a terrible face toward Ma.

Quietly, Ma took a deep breath and said, " 'The locusts have no king, yet go they forth all of them by bands.' Oh, Mary, I am so sorry."

My mouth felt dusty and raw. My stomach hurt. I couldn't even look at Billy. We sat in that dugout, and even the thick walls could not keep out the sound of them chewing, eating up all we'd worked for.

CHAPTER TWENTY

THEY SQUISHED UNDER MY FEET. I slid a little and Billy put out an arm to steady me. He looked green—the way I felt. I could see them eating the grass right as we walked over them out to the cornfield. Out to what once *was* a cornfield.

Billy raised his arms and let them drop. "I can't believe it's all gone, Sam, *all* gone. Every little bit of it. How could they be so hungry?"

Every leaf was eaten. Every stem was chawed down to the ground.

"Don't ask me! What I want to know is, where did they come from? And how did they know to come here? Answer me that!"

Billy rubbed his nose. "Don't get mad at me, Sam, it's not my fault we lost everything. Remember what Harold said: 'There's no such thing as always.' "

"Harold! Always!" I choked. I wasn't used to it yet. I still felt sick at my stomach even though they'd been here three days.

Pa came over and joined us, pushing his hat back. "God, I could dynamite those critters!"

Pa swore! In front of us! Billy looked at him with his mouth open.

"You make plans, boys, and think you've got it all worked out. The weather I knew about, the climate I knew about, but grasshoppers!" His face was tight and sour, the way it was on his old dark days. I drew closer to him. What if losing the crop made those bad days come back?

"Couldn't we plow the field and plant it again? Billy and I'd help. We'd work all day and night, if we had to!" I didn't care about my old rifle. I didn't care about getting rich. I just didn't want Pa to look so sad and tired.

Pa squeezed my shoulder. "You are good boys. But it's too late to plant, Sam. Too late," he sighed. "Pete got news from town, and he told me the grasshoppers are hundreds of miles in all directions. And they don't look like leaving soon."

"Will we have to go home, Pa?" Billy whispered.

I started. We couldn't go home, not give up. Not leave the house we'd made!

"I don't know, son, maybe. It took most of what we had to get here. If we stayed, we'd have to buy supplies from town and even then, there's no guarantee the grasshoppers won't be here another year."

Billy looked at me, his eyes shocked. I couldn't say anything.

Pa slouched back to the house, Jake keeping close to his heels. That dog always knew when someone needed comfort. He was so used to the grasshoppers now, he didn't even snap at them.

"Let's go to the creek, Sam," Billy whispered. "Don't want to be in the dugout, somehow."

I nodded, and we set off toward the bluff. When I stepped on the grasshoppers, they gave off a bad smell—a musty, dead smell, I breathed through my mouth all the way to the creek.

We slid down the bank and sat on the rocks. Billy threw a piece of wood into the water. "This is the worst thing that ever happened to us."

"Worse than the war?"

"Well, at least Grandpa had a farm after the soldiers went home. We don't even have a farm."

"Shhh. Pa'll think of something. He'll have to." I watched the grasshoppers in the water. They'd piled up on top of each other trying to get across, and the stream was full of their bodies. The sun beat down on my head. All the leaves were gone, and it was hot and still.

"Even the horses don't want to drink the water." Billy stood and threw a stick. "I hate it out here, Sam. They ate up all the pretty things and left all the ugly things."

The trees were black and spindly over the brown water. The prairie looked dead and squashed. Even the sky was ugly, a kind of smeary gray. My head ached, and we headed back to the dugout.

———————

SOMEBODY HAD TO DO SOMETHING. I looked around the table that night as Ma dished out bean stew. She set down Grandma's flowered bowl filled with the lettuce and carrots she'd saved and sprinkled with vinegar and sugar.

"Somebody has to do something!" I thumped my hand down. "We can't just sit here and let them eat up everything!"

"Hush, Sam," Ma said.

"Well, we can't, Ma. We came all the way West, we worked hard as field hands building this farm, and look at it!"

"I know that, Sam," Pa smoothed his beard down. It worried me that he did it again and again. "But what can we do? Fire doesn't keep them away. Nothing scares them. They're a plague, like in the Bible. We have to wait until the plague goes away. Then we'll see what we shall see." He smiled at me, but his eyes were dark and tired.

"How will we feed the horses now the grass is gone? How will we buy seed for next year if we can't sell a crop?" I rubbed my knuckles under the table.

"We'll find a way, Sam." Ma pursed her lips.

"Maybe we'll have to ask Grandpa for money," Billy said slowly, patting Jake's head.

"No!" Pa slammed his hand on the table. "I won't go asking the colonel for money. We either have to make it on our own—or not." He rubbed his beard.

"You mean, go back home?" Billy asked in a small voice.

Ma fidgeted with her napkin. Jake thumped his tail against the floor and put his head back down when no one patted him.

Suddenly, I jumped up and opened the door. "I'm not going to just sit here and let them take everything. I'm going to *do* something!" I ran outside. No one followed.

Stars sprinkled the sky like the sugar on Ma's lettuce. Ham and Duke stamped in the field. They were hungry. A tiny moon hung over the bare trees by the creek. I held my head back and felt something wet slipping down my cheeks. I opened my mouth, wanting to howl like a wolf. Instead, I ran over to

Duke and pressed my face against his chest. He smelled good—not like grasshoppers. He nuzzled my neck and whickered softly. Duke knew. I smelled that sweet horse smell and thought of home—Grandma and Grandpa on the porch, sipping lemonade. All this time I'd missed them, and now we might be going home. Pa said so. But how could I leave the house we'd built, the barn I'd helped make with sod bricks? And how could I leave now I'd found a friend?

Duke nuzzled me again. Somehow I would find a way.

CHAPTER TWENTY-ONE

I TOUCHED MY GOOD-LUCK PIECES IN THE WALL hollow. Billy slept on, like Ma and Pa. The first light came through the window, pink on the table. How could it be so pretty when everything had gone wrong?

I rubbed the fossil stone. I could trap animals this winter and sell furs in the spring. There were muskrat, otter, and mink along the creek; all of them should bring something in. But how much? Enough to let us stay?

I looked at Billy and wanted to shake him. How could he sleep so calm and quiet?

Grandpa gave me twenty-five cents when I left. I touched the coin in the hollow. With that and trapping money, I could give Pa maybe six to eight dollars. That wouldn't do much! We'd need money for seed come spring, and money for supplies to get us through the winter. There was only one thing I could think of, and I didn't like it. I tossed and turned until everyone finally got up. Ma chided me for fidgeting at the table, but I couldn't sit still and ran outside to stand on top of the dugout. It was like being a sentry at the fort up there; I could see danger coming, or at least *think* about it and prepare for it. Jake stood beside me, ears cocked, almost like he was watching with me.

It was still early in the day when I saw somebody running toward me. He waved a hat and shouted, and I knew it was Allan.

"Whooh, Allan!" I waved my hat at him.

He ran up to me and stood, sweat rolling down his red face. "Don't you just hate this, Sam?" He kicked at the grasshoppers with his foot.

We looked out over the land—brown and flat. Brown grasshoppers crawled over it.

"I hate it, but it isn't doing me much good. Grasshoppers don't care if I hate them!" I scuffed at them with my foot, and Jake wiggled and whined beside me.

"What're your folks going to do?" Allan took his hat off, wiped his brow, and jammed it on again. "Do you know?"

"Not yet, Allan. Some days it looks like Pa'll stay. Other days he talks at supper about going home again and doing the 'sensible' thing, he calls it."

"Same as my pa. Like a weathervane blowing yes, no, yes, no."

"We've got to find a way to help them stay, Allan," I said fiercely. "We can't go home after all we put into this land. Building the dugout—why, we cut the bricks for it." I knelt and patted the sod roof. "We laid them up and helped dig out the hill. We hauled willow brush from the creek for the roof. We poked holes in the sod with sticks to plant the corn." I was breathing hard, and it made me hot.

"I know," Allan sighed. "Same as I did. Worked side by side with Pa. It's *our* farm. But what can we do, Sam? We can't get work, and it's too early to start trapping fur animals."

"Is there anybody back home who can help you out?" I kicked the grasshoppers aside and sat, hugging my knees. At least there was a breeze up here to dry the sweat.

"Nope. Everybody else went West, too, and Grandpa and Grandma died a few years back. They didn't have much, anyway." Allan knelt and rubbed Jake's ears. "Oh, I do love the way this dog smells. Only thing around here that doesn't smell of grasshoppers. Do you want to go fishing?" He looked up.

"No. They all taste of grasshoppers." I spat.

"There's only one thing to do, Allan. I can't tell Pa about it; he'd whip me if he knew."

"What, Sam? What're you going to do?"

I sighed. I did hate to admit we couldn't do it on our own. "Write Grandpa and tell him what happened. It's the only way."

Allan stood. "Then I'll write Washington."

"Washington! How can you do that?"

Allan pursed his lips. "Don't know. I guess if I write a letter and address it to Washington, that somebody'll read it. They should know, Sam. We're their settlers, opening up new territory. They *need* us. It stands to reason they should help us."

My mouth just stayed open. Never, ever, would I write to Washington. It was too faraway. What did those politicians, who Grandpa said were sewn up out of a pig's backside, care about us settlers out on the prairies? You asked your folks for help; you didn't ask faraway people.

"You write your letter—I'll write mine," Allan said. "Do you have some paper and pens? We could do it now."

I ran inside and asked Ma. "Allan and I are going to practice—practice our writing, Ma. Do you have some old paper and pens? We want to try real writing, not on slates."

Ma beamed at us. "That's my good boy. Here."

She found some paper and gave me a pen and her tiny inkwell. "Be careful. There's not much ink left."

I ran out and called to Allan. "Come down by the barn. It's cooler there."

I took a shovel and scraped two places clean so we wouldn't have to *sit* on them, and we put our backs against the sod barn. It felt good to have that solid wall at my back, a wall I had helped build.

I rested the paper on one of Ma's magazines. "Dear Grandpa," I began. "Maybe you have heard of what happened out here. How the grasshoppers came and ate up all we planted. Even my fishing pole is yellow as they ate the wood off. Ma is pale and tired, and Pa hardly says anything anymore. Billy and I want to help them but don't know how. So I am writing to you, Grandpa, to ask for help. Pa wouldn't allow it if he knew. If I could borrow—"

I dipped my pen into the inkwell and sighed. "How much money will we need, Allan? For seed next year?"

"Well, we'll plant wheat next year. Ask for fifty dollars just to be safe. You'll need to buy supplies from the station, too."

"I know," I snapped. So much money!

"If I could borrow"— the pen sputtered—"fifty dollars, that would pay for supplies and seed for next year. If you could send more, we could loan some to our good neighbors, the Grants, so they could stay, too. But I know that fifty dollars is a lot of money. When cold weather comes, I'll set some traps for mink, otter, and muskrat. Maybe in—" I stopped.

"How long will it take to pay back fifty dollars, Allan?"

Allan counted on his fingers. "I don't know, Sam. A couple of years, anyway."

I dipped the pen into the ink and thought. By trapping and hiring out, I could earn ten dollars or more a year. "I hope in five years I can finish paying you back. And here is my mark to seal this promise, Grandpa."

I took out my penknife, jabbed it into my thumb until the blood rose up, and dabbed it on the paper. I let it dry to a dull brown, folded the paper crossways and then lengthwise, and addressed the envelope to Grandpa.

I handed the pen to Allan. "Now you write."

"How do I start, Sam? 'Dear Sirs?' 'Dear Politicians?' 'Dear Fathers of the Country?' " He pushed his hat back.

" 'Dear Sirs,' I think."

"Dear Sirs. Maybe you don't know yet what's happened out here in Dakota Territory and everywhere to the west, south, and east of us, too, dear sirs. The grasshoppers they came and et everything up. There's nothing left. Not a grass not a stick not a tree. We're bare as bare. And no one knows how to get through the winter. Most of us borrowed to get here and buy the seed. How will we plant next year? How can we settle the land if you don't help? Please send us money and blankets and seed corn and wheat and maybe a book or two to keep the mothers happy. Your servant, Allan Grant, age twelve."

I didn't say anything at first. Asking for blankets! It looked like charity to me, and if there was one thing Pa hated, it was charity.

"It's all true, Sam, what I wrote." Allan fiddled with the pen.

"That's right. It is a true story, and how can we get in trouble for telling the truth? That's what Harold always said."

He wanted to know who Harold was, so I told him about Harold and Grandma and Grandpa, and our white house with the wide porch and breezes, and the grave where Billy buried Eleanor. I told him about Luke and Jeb and fishing in the catfish river, and how much I hated school. I felt like I was unloading a box full of heavy packages, and after I told him about home, I felt clean and light like an empty box.

Allan sighed and stood up. "I've got to get home and help Pa. I just came to see if you were staying or going."

"Could you mail this for me, or get your pa to do

it?" I asked. "If they saw I was writing to Grandpa, they might guess, and Pa'd tear up the letter. Does your Ma have gum seal for letters?"

" 'Course she does." Allan took the letter and tucked it in his shirt pocket.

I ran inside, took Grandpa's quarter from the wall niche, and gave it to Allan for mailing the letter. "I'm not sure what a letter costs, Allan, but just give me the change—if there is any—next time we meet."

Allan put his hat on and patted his shirt pocket. "We done what we could, Sam, can't do more, as Pa says. Either they help us or they don't."

CHAPTER TWENTY-TWO

"I'M GOING INTO TOWN TODAY." Pa stood after breakfast and put on his new yellow straw hat. "I'll see what the news is. Maybe there's work on the railroad, Ellie."

"Of course." Ma patted his shoulders and straightened his hat. "There's bound to be something, Walt. We'll get by, you'll see."

"Yes, Ellie." He kissed her, but missed her cheek. You could tell his mind was somewhere else.

Billy and I harnessed Duke to the wagon and handed the reins to Pa.

"Thanks, boys. You take care of your mother now. And don't worry!" He leaned out and gave

Billy's chin a little shake. Slapping the reins, he stood and waved as the wagon rolled away.

"That's a good sign," I whispered to Billy.

"What is?"

"Standing up and waving. He does that when he's feeling better."

"Well, I wish he'd decide soon, Sam. I can't stand this waiting around much longer!" Billy swatted his shoe with a stick. His face was red from the heat.

"William! It's not for us to decide, it's Pa's—"

"Why is it!" He turned and faced me, breathing hard. "Why is it Pa's decision? Didn't we help plant that big cornfield? Didn't we help load sod bricks and lay them up for the house? Didn't we help with the barn? Well?"

I sat down suddenly, not minding what I squished. "Well, yes."

"Then we should help decide, and I say we should stay."

Jake nuzzled his hand, but Billy didn't notice. Two hawks wheeled high overhead, and the swallows dipped and fluttered.

"Going south soon," Billy whispered. "Hope we're not going with them."

———————————

ALL THAT DAY WE HELPED MA IN THE DUGOUT. We swept down the newspaper walls and took the

———

146

cookstove outside. Billy cleaned it with a brush, and I polished it up. We brought willow brush from the creek and wove it over the rafters in places that needed it. And when we slept that night and the next with Pa gone, I kept waking and looking at the darkness. What was Pa doing? Had he found anything? What would we do if Grandpa didn't send the money?

The roof curved over me. I could feel the prairie stretching away overhead. I could feel the poor, eaten trees down by the creek, their roots going deep into the earth—looking for a home.

Two days after Pa left, it was hot as ever, with the wind blowing little dust clouds along the prairie. The sky was gray and smoky.

"Maybe it'll rain," Billy sighed.

"Maybe." I'd stopped hoping that the heat would break.

We went to the barn and cleaned it, though Pa always left things pretty neat. We oiled Ham's harness and hung it back on the wall. Billy put oil on all the tool handles, which were yellow now.

"I can't believe they ate all the old wood off, Sam. There's something not natural about them—not right. It makes me feel sick."

"I know, Billy, but we just have to keep going."

"Like Harold did." Billy rubbed oil into the long reins.

I almost spat out, "Harold!" But then I thought,

he *did* just keep going. Learning to read, planning to send for his wife, making a new life for himself. Maybe Harold felt like his things were always getting eaten up by grasshoppers. And we were luckier because we only got the grasshoppers once.

"Hear that, Sam?" Billy ran to the door and looked out. The sky was filled with towering, black clouds.

"Thunder!" Lightning zigzagged across the sky, and the rain fell in great, fat drops.

"Hurry!" I shouted. "Back to the dugout!"

We ran through the rain, but got slower and slower until we stopped by the door. The wet washed down my head, my eyes, the sweat from my face. I stripped off my shirt and pants. Billy laughed and did the same. The door flew open, and Ma ran out carrying buckets to catch the rain.

"Here! Soap! Now we don't have to drink and bathe in that awful creek water!" She unpinned her hair and it tumbled down in the rain. We soaped up each other's backs, and Ma washed her hair, singing. Her dress was covered with white suds. Billy danced, holding his arms up to the rain.

The air tingled, and the hairs on my arms rose. "Quick, inside!" I pulled on Billy's and Ma's hands, hurrying them through the door.

A huge crack of thunder sounded.

"Whooee! Sam, how did you know that was coming?" Billy wiped his eyes with a towel.

"I could feel it on my arms."

Ma hugged me tight, then laughed. "Oh, I don't care, somehow. I've got soap in my eyes, and my hair is wringing wet, and the lightning almost got us, and I don't care!

"Don't you see, boys?" Ma sat at the table and rubbed her wet hair. "It's a promise. New grass will grow, and we can feed the horses. It will wash out that dead smell, and maybe the grasshoppers will go away."

"Maybe, Ma." Billy patted her arms dry with his towel.

The door flew open, and Pa leaped inside, slamming it behind. "Whew! That last one almost got me!"

"Walter!" Ma jumped up and hugged him. "If I'd known you were out in that storm—"

"But you were out in it—you're all wet and soapy," he laughed. He sat at the table and pulled a cheroot out from his coat. "Kept this dry, thank goodness." He lit it slowly, puffed, took it out of his mouth and looked at it, then put it back into his mouth.

"Well?" Billy said.

"Well?" I stood behind him, smelling that good smoke.

"You won't believe the things I saw." He sucked in some smoke and let it seep out the corners of his mouth. "Wagons and people and families going home.

A lot of folks are pulling up stakes and leaving, Ellie."

Ma stopped smiling and rubbed her arms.

"They've got things painted on their wagons. " 'West Isn't Best!' 'Broke, Going Home!' And no one's got enough to eat." His smile died. "I tell you, Ellie, it's enough to make a man . . ." He stopped. Jake thumped his tail once and was still. My throat dried, waiting for his next words.

"But we just can't do that, Ellie, Sam, and Billy. We worked too hard to get here and make this farm, and by gosh, we're not going home." He thumped his fist on the table. "I don't care what we have to do. I'm not going back to Kentucky and that old, worn-out earth. This is good earth here—a little eaten"—he smiled—"but good, rich earth."

"But how can we stay, Pa?" Billy leaned against his other shoulder.

"I've taken out a loan from the bank, son. I talked with the banker when I was in town, and you can borrow money from them to buy seed the next year."

"Borrow money?" Ma twisted her hands.

"I know, Ellie. I don't like it, but it's either that or go home to your folks, and I just can't do that."

Billy let out a long sigh. I squeezed Pa's shoulder so tight he said, "Ouch! Sam!" He puffed on his cheroot and handed it to me. "Want to try it, son?"

Slowly, I took it and sucked on the wet end. The thick, sharp smoke filled my mouth, went up my nose. I coughed and gave it back. Pa handed it to Billy.

"Want to try, William?"

Billy took it carefully and breathed in some smoke. He coughed, gasped, and handed it back to Pa.

The dugout was thick with Pa's smoke. We all were wet and shivering. But I felt like a fire was lit inside my stomach and it could never be put out.

CHAPTER TWENTY-THREE

A FEW DAYS AFTER PA CAME BACK FROM TOWN with the loan and the promise that we would stay, Billy and I were taking a bucketful of grasshoppers outdoors to dump to the side—where we always did. Because every time we went inside, *they* came with us. And Ma just wouldn't tolerate having them in the house.

"Sam! Do you see what I see?" Billy dumped the bucket out and pushed his hat back. He shaded his eyes.

"What?" I kicked at the smelly pile.

"They're moving."

"Who is? Speak up, can't you?"

"Why, the grasshoppers, Sam!" he said reproach-fully.

I took my hat off and ran up to the top of the dugout. It was quiet as quiet. No sound of them eating. They were walking across the land, like a huge brown army. Walking, walking, one behind another. The ground crawled.

"Ma!" Billy screamed. "Pa! Come look! Quick!" Pa came running from the barn, and Ma ran out of the dugout, her face worried.

"What is it, William? Are you hurt?" She peered into his face.

"No, Ma! Look at the grasshoppers!"

She and Pa stood behind us, watching. Ma gasped, "Oh, my! Will you look at that!"

Pa seized her hand and jigged up and down. "They're moving, Ellie, moving on!"

Side by side, wings touching wings, they marched across the prairie. They came up across the dugout, crawling up Pa's pants legs and Ma's dress.

"Quick, inside!" Pa herded us into the dugout.

"Oooh, oooh!" Ma shivered, brushing the grass-hoppers off. Pa squished them with a shovel and kept the door open. He killed them with that shovel when they came in the door.

"Look at them!" Billy waved his fists. "They're leaving. Those miserable, godforsaken . . ."

"Billy! Don't swear!"

"But they *are* miserable, Ma."

"*And* godforsaken," Pa said loudly.

"And low-down, mean, disgusting creatures," I spat. Jake barked and ran outside, running in crazy circles. He knew!

"And they're leaving!" we all shouted together. We took each other's hands and danced around the dugout, chanting, "They're going, they're leaving for good, hallelujah, Oh, hallelujah!" It was like a prayer and a song, and we said it over and over again. Ma's face was like a girl's, with no worry lines, and Pa kept shouting, "Hallelujah!"

He pulled us outside. "We have to see this, even if they get in our clothes."

A dry, raspy sound started up, a big chirring. The armies of grasshoppers moved faster and faster, lifting into the air in a brown, whistling cloud. We all crouched to the ground, and Jake dropped behind us, whining. Up, up over the dugout, up away from the creek, up into the greasy sky off to the west. They made a funny, hard sound when they flew, and Ma put her hands to her ears. The sky was brown with their bodies, brown like the bottom of a pot where something burned and smelled bad. They kept going over us, and the horses stomped and whinnied in the stable.

"Ham and Duke are glad, too," I said.

I don't know how long we stood there watching. Could've been a few minutes—or an hour. Finally, the sky was clear, the brown gone. Pa sighed. Ma wiped her eyes on the corner of her apron, and Billy and I let out two loud war whoops.

"They're gone," Ma whispered. "They're gone. Now, maybe we can begin to live again."

CHAPTER TWENTY-FOUR

ALL THAT WEEK WE CUT HAY IN THE SLOUGH for winter feed for Ham and Duke. The slough was a pie-shaped piece of land covered with thick, tall grass. It was about the only thing the grasshoppers *didn't* eat, maybe because it was so coarse. Pa cut the grass with his scythe, and Billy and I turned the hay to dry with our pitchforks. Every day we had lemonade and bread in the shade of the wagon, and I wondered were the Grants staying or not? I was too busy to visit, and Allan didn't come to our dugout. It made me nervous, thinking that they must be going, and that Mr. Grant was keeping Allan busy all that week getting ready.

I kept asking Pa if he was going into town to get the mail, but he always answered the same: "Not till the hay is in, Sam. Besides, what's the hurry?" I couldn't tell him about the letter I was waiting for. But I had it worked out in my mind; now we had money from the bank to help us stay, we could loan Grandpa's money—if he sent it—to the Grants to help *them* stay.

We took the last load of hay back and stopped by the sod barn. It was hot, and the sweat trickled into my eyes. The rain we had a week ago didn't cool it off much, but new grass was popping up all over the prairie. It looked like a green wave spreading, and I wondered if good things were like a tide; they came in and were sucked away. But they always came back.

Billy and I forked the hay down to Pa, who made wide, tall stacks. I heard a shout.

"Halloo, Whites!"

The Grants were all sitting in their wagon, dressed like partygoers. Amanda held Ben on her lap, both in blue bonnets, and Mrs. Grant had on a fresh, yellow sunbonnet. Even Allan had on new suspenders.

I took off my hat. Were they dressed up to go? Allan never looked like that.

Billy grabbed my arm. "They're leaving, Sam. You can tell. Amanda never wears a sunbonnet unless it's something special."

Ma came out of the dugout, wiping her hands. She ran up to the wagon. "Oh, Mary, you're not going—not now, without ever a visit or a last chance to. . . ." She dropped her hands.

Mrs. Grant slid to the ground and hugged Ma tight. "Good-bye, Ellen, good-bye." Her eyes were squeezed tight shut over Ma's shoulder. "We had to leave like this. I just couldn't bear to come visiting, knowing we were going and all."

Allan jumped down from the wagon back and took my hand. He shook it so hard my arm ached. "Good-bye, Sam, good-bye. I thought we might hear from Washington by now, but we didn't. Guess those politicians don't care much about us settlers."

"Hush, Allan!" Mrs. Grant opened her eyes.

"But, Ma—"

"Just hush!" I guess being sad made Mrs. Grant crabby.

Mr. Grant seized Pa's hand and shook it. "You've been good neighbors, Walt, and we will miss you."

"I wish you could stay, Pete. I hate to see you go. Isn't there some way? Would you borrow money from the bank?"

"No, Walter, we've already borrowed money, and the interest is too high out here. We just have to go." He took his hat off and wiped his face. "But we'll be back. Soon as we save enough money, we're coming back here! Not all the land will be settled up, especially not after these pesky grasshoppers!"

"I'm so glad they're gone," Mrs. Grant sighed.

Billy talked to Amanda in the wagon, and she laughed. I guessed Billy would always make the girls laugh, and women would always say, "Oh, that Billy," until he was about one hundred years old. And I'd never figure out what it was that made women like him so.

"This is for you." Mr. Grant took a letter out of his shirt pocket and handed it to me. I almost dropped it.

"Me?" It was here—at last.

"Well, go on, open it!" Allan said. "Open it!"

The paper crackled in my hand. The sweat from my palms made the ink run, and I could just make out the address to "Master Samuel T. White, Bancroft, Dakota Territory."

"Samuel T. White." That made me stand up straighter, and carefully, I opened the letter.

"Dear Sam," it read, "I received your letter and was moved by your description of your family. We can't have Ellen looking pale and worn, nor have your father tired. And much as I want you here, home with Grandma and me, we can't have your new life in a new land blighted because of a plague of locusts. I am sending fifty dollars to you to help buy seed for the next year. We don't have more money to help your friends. I will hold you to your bargain, that in five years you will pay me back. However you earn the money does not matter, as long as you fulfill your bargain."

I could just see him, writing that, sitting tall and straight in his hickory chair by the fireplace. I could almost hear the sound of his bugle in the distance, and I stood even straighter.

"Kiss your mother for me, and all the rest. Your loving grandfather, William."

"Well?" Ma pushed at her sunbonnet. "What does he say, Sam? And why is he writing to you? I don't understand this at all."

"He sent us this." I held out fifty dollars, in ten-dollar bills.

"What?" Pa strode forward and seized the money, holding it up to the light. "Fifty dollars! From the colonel. Sam!" He turned on me. "What did you do? Did you go asking Grandpa for money when I said we weren't going to?"

"Yes, he did send me the money, Pa. I asked for it, 'cause I knew you wouldn't, and somebody had to make plans for the future." I faced him and breathed as hard as he did. "I didn't know then about the bank—when I wrote. And I just couldn't let us go home again, not after Billy and me helped build our house and barn and hauled buckets of dirt and poked holes in the sod to plant corn and all." I sucked in a breath. "Somebody had to do something, don't you see?"

Pa stared at me, his mouth tight. "I said . . ." He stopped.

"Hush, Walter." Ma patted his arm. "Sam did what he thought was right, and that's all any of us can ever do."

Pa stepped back. Ma came up behind him, and Billy stood on my other side.

"And I'm going to pay him back! We made a bargain, Grandpa and me." I scratched Jake's head. He was warm and solid under my hand. I didn't say that it made me nervous thinking about paying Grandpa back, and that fifty dollars was a lot of money, and could I trap enough animals?

Ma smiled at me, and it got broader and broader. "Well, well, will you think of that. Sam asking Grandpa. Sam paying Grandpa back." She hugged me tight.

"Walter," Mr. Grant said. "The boy did what he thought was right. And he's not such a boy anymore, is he?"

"Take the money." Pa held the bills out to Mr. Grant. "There's enough here. Besides, I've got money from the bank."

I looked at Allan, and he grabbed my arm.

Mr. Grant pulled on his beard. "Walter, we can't.

We can't take money from a friend. But we'll be back, just you wait!" He helped Mrs. Grant onto the seat, Allan jumped in back, and the reins flapped on the horses. The wagon began to roll.

Billy and I ran beside it. "It didn't help, Allan."

"Hush!" Allan jammed his hat on. "You tried, and I tried, and that's all anybody can ever do, Sam. I'll see you next year, or the year after. *Then* you'll see some fishing. *Then* we'll go hunting with that pony and rifle of yours."

I waved to baby Ben, who looked as solemn as ever in his blue bonnet. Amanda waved, and Billy took off his hat and swept it back and forth. "Good-bye!" he yelled.

My eyes blurred as the wagon pulled away from me. Allan was gone, and Pa was mad at me. Dust rose in little spurts and disappeared into the sky.

CHAPTER TWENTY-FIVE

A MONTH LATER, THE WEATHER TURNED. The warm breeze disappeared, and a cold one swept down from the north. Ham and Duke turned their backs to it, tails blowing in the wind. Jake kept close inside by the stove, which Ma kept going all day now.

We went into town to get supplies for the winter. I smiled, watching Ma. Her flowered purse held the money from Grandpa, and I thought of the food we were buying as mine.

"My arms are coming out of my sleeves," Billy said, helping me lift a sack of flour into the wagon.

"So're mine!" I held them next to Billy's. *Mine* were longer!

"You both have grown." Pa settled the sacks of beans, sugar, tea, and coffee on the wagon floor. Then he lifted in the barrel of salt pork.

"Did you hear what the storekeeper said?" Ma asked us. "The government is sending aid to us settlers—barrels of food, clothing, and blankets."

Billy stared at me. "Too late for the Grants!"

"They wouldn't have taken it, I bet," I said.

"Charity!" Pa grimaced.

"No, it's not, Walter. They must help us, for we're helping them."

But I noticed that Pa never called that money from Grandpa charity, and he never said another word to me about it. That wasn't his way. Not even when he helped me set my traps down by the creek.

ONE NIGHT I WOKE UP AND HEARD THE QUIETest kind of silence. It pressed in on my ears, louder than any noise. An owl called, "Hoo-whoah, whoo-whoah," and I shivered, curling closer to Billy.

When I opened the door the next morning, the air pinched my nose. Snow covered the ground and hid all the ripples and hollows. In some places, it was purple or blue.

Ma was feeding kindling into the stove box. "It snowed, Sam! This is your first snow." Like it was a present she was giving me.

"Yes, Ma." I grabbed my jacket and shoes and went outside, thinking I'd help Pa with the horses. Instead, I climbed to the top of the dugout, the place where I'd seen so much. Here we'd watched the grasshoppers come homing in—that great, whistling cloud. I'd watched for mail from the top of the dugout, hoping Grandpa's money would save us all and keep the Grants from going home. And here I'd watched the Grants leave, their wagon wheels rolling across the prairie. I wondered what Allan was doing back home.

I walked out to the cornfield, saw how empty it looked, and then looped down to the creek. Snow lay on the black branches. I remembered Billy sitting on the rock and saying, "They ate up all the pretty things and left all the ugly things, Sam." Not everyone had a brother who could think like that.

When I neared the house, Billy poked his head out of the door and shouted, "What're you doing, Sam? It snowed, did you see that? Our first snow! Better than Kentucky, hey?" He scooped some up and took a big bite.

I waved and then looked back at the tracks I'd made. They circled from our roof out to the field, to the creek, the sod barn, and back to our home inside the earth. Once Billy told me Harold thought circles could be magic. That you could make a safe line round something or somebody you wanted to protect from harm.

I wished on my tracks. I prayed to the sky I didn't think was safe to protect us—if not for always, at least through next year, through the next crop. I asked that my steps in the snow would keep Pa, Ma, Billy, me, and Jake safe, and don't forget the horses, either, and that next spring the wheat would come up and Allan might come back. And if we were lucky, we'd make enough money to send for Ma's organ. Then I changed that. "Forget the organ," I said. "Just keep us together."

"Are you talking to yourself, Samuel T. White?" Billy rolled his eyes and hunched his shoulders.

"Oh, you!" I hurled myself forward and tackled him in the door. And I wrestled him just a bit longer after Ma turned from the stove and said, "William! Sam! Come to breakfast this minute!"